I've travelled the world twice over,
Met the famous: saints and sinners,
Poets and artists, kings and queens,
Old stars and hopeful beginners,
I've been where no-one's been before,
Learned secrets from writers and cooks
All with one library ticket
To the wonderful world of books.

© JANICE JAMES.

SOMEONE LYING, SOMEONE DYING

The remains of Walter Blythe are found in the cellar, and the awkward questions begin. What had happened to the £10,000 Walter had supposedly cheated from his partner? Have the 'respectable' Johnson's been profiting from it — and if so, what restitution can be made since there are no descendants? No descendants — first Pietro, brash and offensive, turns up from Sicily, and then another claimant with an equally plausible story emerges. But who, if any, is telling the truth?

JONATHAN BURKE

SOMEONE LYING, SOMEONE DYING

F/405048

Complete and Unabridged

ULVERSCROFT
Leicester

First published in Great Britain in 1968

First Large Print Edition
published December 1991

British Library CIP Data

Burke, Jonathan *1922–*
Someone lying, someone dying. — Large print ed. —
Ulverscroft large print series: mystery
I. Title
823.914 [F] ▮▮▮▮▮▮

ISBN 0–7089–2549–9

Published by
F. A. Thorpe (Publishing) Ltd.
Anstey, Leicestershire
Set by Words & Graphics Ltd.
Anstey, Leicestershire
Printed and bound in Great Britain by
T. J. Press (Padstow) Ltd., Padstow, Cornwall

1

THEY stood at the rear window of the bare, bright room and watched dust and smoke rising from the demolition site a hundred yards away. In here was the smell of new paint. Wood and metal and the white ceiling shone. Out there, the tired grey walls flinched and sagged under the assault of picks, ropes and a bulldozer. Here a beginning; there an end.

Martin said: "I suppose they'll be doing that to this place, one day."

"We haven't even moved in yet!" Brigid protested.

Men balanced on the raw ends of girders, chopping out bricks. After a while they attached a rope from a bulldozer and scrambled away. The throb of the engine pounded across the site and made the windows of the flat vibrate. The yellow monster strained like a massive horse against the taut rope. It shuddered forward, churning up the earth, until the

1

wall of the building fell gently outwards
and dissolved. A breeze blew up the hill
from the sea, puffing a pall of dust in
slow motion across the ruins. Grit settled
on the blossom of the two trees at the
end of the garden. Once there had been a
smooth lawn; now there was a mish-mash
of bulldozer and heavy lorry tracks.

Brigid glanced at Martin. He was
absorbed in the remorseless process of
destruction.

She liked to have the chance, every now
and then, of studying him when he wasn't
aware of her. She tried to see him as a
stranger; tried to say 'There's a rather
gorgeous man, I wonder what he's like,
I wonder what his mouth is like when he
smiles — rather stiff now, as though he's
got something on his mind and is very,
very slightly talking to himself, but I bet
I could make those lips soften — and
I wonder what he's thinking about and
whether I can attract his attention and
make him think about me.'

He was frowning. From here she
couldn't see his right eye but she knew
that it would be wider than the left,
quizzical and demanding, just as it was

when he was about to bend over his microscope and watch weird little things wiggling about on a glass slide. Now he watched the men swarming over the demolition site. With her own eyes shut she could lovingly have traced the line of his profile: the oddly jutting, aggressive peak of fair hair above his bony forehead, and the almost Etruscan nose, dominating yet not quite defeating the mouth she now knew so well.

Brigid felt a twinge of impatience. She had had her fill of contemplation. It was time he came back to her. If he was thinking anything interesting, she wanted him to share it with her.

Perhaps, with that self-mocking solemnity which was so much a part of him, he was seeing a parallel between their own lives and the activity outside. Brigid was growing into the habit of anticipating his thoughts and trying to match them. Our separate lives, she now ventured, each being pulled apart so that something fresh can be constructed on the débris. A month from now we'll be living here. Living together.

She had said this over and over again

to herself recently and still found it hard to believe. Living here. With Martin. Married, and settled in this flat. Part of each other, and each of them a part of something else.

She longed to make him turn to her and smile. At the same time she felt a quickening of fear at the prospect of surrendering her freedom. She didn't have to pretend that he was a stranger: he *was* a stranger. To him perhaps she, too, was a stranger.

She said: "Everything seems to be going ahead so . . . so implacably, doesn't it?"

"Everything?" he said vaguely, still engrossed.

"The arrangements," she said: "the presents and the cake and the reception and the new carpets and the furniture and the business of turning on the electricity and the gas and . . . oh, everything."

He nodded.

"Do you want to turn back before it's too late?" said Brigid.

Flame licked up through the emptiness of a window. Workmen threw planks and the jagged remains of panelling on to a fire

4

carefully shielded in the open cellars of the house. The writhing pattern of flame, smoke and dust changed ceaselessly.

At last Martin faced her, giving her his full attention and speaking only after the usual fractional delay during which he analysed what had been said to him. "I don't think I could be rebuilt as a separate entity now."

"Not a very romantic way of putting it."

He slid his arm round her. They leaned against the pillar that divided the long window into two segments and lazily swayed to face the room.

Their flat was on the second floor of a new block built by her father's company. The sitting room which had looked so small on the plan and not much larger while the block was being erected now showed up as a spacious, well-proportioned room. It ran from front to back of the building and had one attractively eccentric arm turning sharply along the rear wall, enfolding a boxroom. In an apparently confined space the architect had been able to fit two bedrooms, bathroom, kitchen and this inner boxroom. At the moment it was all, really, an abstraction. Brigid and Martin were standing not in their home but in what the planners called 'living space' — well designed and organised, but nothing more than space in which no-one had yet done any living.

Carpets and furniture would make a difference when they arrived. The wear and tear of everyday existence would make a difference.

Being married to Martin and living here with him would make a difference.

Brigid said: "Where shall we put the couch — along that wall, or opposite the heater?"

"I don't mind."

"But where do you think it would fit in best?"

Martin gave this a few seconds' reluctant consideration and said: "Wherever we put it, you'll be moving it around for weeks before we finally settle."

"Will I?"

"Women do."

"Do they?"

"So I've been told. When they're first

6

married. And once a year at spring-cleaning time."

"Is this the voice of personal experience? Your mother has an annual shake-up?"

"No, it doesn't happen to us, I'll admit. Mum likes things to stay in their appointed places." He spoke of his mother with a fondness quite free from uncomfortable sentimentality. "She keeps our rooms the way they were when my father was alive. It's just that she prefers them that way."

"And mine . . . "

"Oh, yours," he said automatically, then stopped.

"What about her?"

"It's rather different."

"Why is it different?"

"Every time I visit you she's got something new."

"Martin, don't exaggerate."

"I have a picture of her falling for something in a shop, ordering it to be delivered at an exact time on a certain day, and then hurrying home to work out her plan of campaign. This piece to be moved over there, that piece over here. Bring this forward, send that back to the rear. And in marches the latest acquisition, slap into the space reserved for it. Banishment for some, advancement for others. For a few months, anyway."

"Martin!"

He let his arm slip away from her shoulders and paced out into the middle of the room, swerving on the way as though to avoid an invisible table.

"There isn't any point in discussing where we'll put our things" — his hand sketched shapes in emptiness, conjuring up a sideboard against one wall and then dismissing it — "when you know perfectly well she'll make all the decisions for us."

"She only wants to help."

"I know. I just wish . . . "

"What?"

"Oh, it's nothing. They're both being awfully good, I know. Don't mind me."

He had reached the window at the other end of the room. His shape was a blur against the dazzle of the sky and the reflected light from the sea and white houses below.

Brigid said: "But I do mind you."

All the other fears and hesitancies about

their marriage were nothing. She was sure everyone had silly little doubts at a time like this. Everyone fluttered and panicked during these last few weeks. But in her case there was this deeper disturbance. She didn't want the surface ripples to be lashed at some unpredictable time into a storm.

Her father ran the largest firm of building contractors in Lurgate. It was indeed the largest for many miles around. He was Johnson of Johnson's, son of the founder. In one of his more prickly moods Martin had said that if Arthur Johnson didn't own half the town he had at least built half of it, and if he had his way he'd pull down the other half and start all over again. It was only natural that when his daughter wanted to get married he should set aside for her and her husband one of the best flats in a new block. From the back windows they would look out on a stretch of communal garden trimly enclosed by garages, and, when the demolition was completed and a new building erected, on another block of bright new flats just close enough to be neighbourly but not so close as to be oppressive. From the front they could look over the roofs tilting down towards the sea. It was every young married couple's dream. Silly not to be grateful; silly not to accept with a good grace.

Brigid followed Martin and stood beside him as he stared down on the steep streets which, in this haze of April light, seemed to plunge straight into the water.

"I do mind," she insisted. "Darling, you're not still being bristly about it, are you? I thought we'd gone over all that. I thought it was all right now."

Many times they had gone over it. Was it going to be always with them? He accepted the logic of it all but his stubborn pride wouldn't give him any peace. He had a good job, but not good enough to pay for a place like this. And if he couldn't pay for it himself he wasn't happy at the idea of living in it. Brigid's father had been very tactful, appreciating that Martin should want to support Brigid in his own way; and Martin liked him for it and did his best to accept, but could not help scratching away at this irritation.

"If I find a better job," he said; "if we have to move away . . . "

"If we have to move away, we move. But what's wrong with enjoying ourselves here while we're here? Mummy and Daddy would buy us an expensive present whatever happened. If it wasn't this flat, it'd be something else."

"I suppose so." Martin put his forehead against the glass. "I'd be pretty unreasonable if I condemned you to life in a cheap back room just because I felt snooty about taking things from your parents. No reason why you should suffer from my pangs of conscience."

"Conscience?"

"Oh, you know what I mean. There'll be all the sour old tongues in the town saying I'm on to a good thing . . . "

"And aren't you?" She took his hand. His fingers tightened on hers.

"Yes," he said. "I'm on to a good thing. You. Because it's you I'm in love with, and nothing to do with anything else."

"So what does anyone else's opinion matter?"

Martin glared down at the streets as though daring anyone to whisper.

The arc of the sea-front road curled out to the end of the bluff, a plump arm of land sheltering the bay. The short pier bisected the arc. Sunlight sparked from the ornate roof of the pavilion. The tide was out and the sand was golden but there were few people on it: the season would not begin in earnest until Easter. A fortnight from now there would be a tangle of cars and coaches on the sea front. Now a blue saloon heading in to the town was able to reach the foot of the hill without halts or hesitations. It turned up towards the block of flats. Brigid recognised it before Martin spoke.

"Here's your mother."

His fingers gripped painfully.

Brigid said: "Darling, she only wants us to be comfortable. She just wants to help."

"I know I promise to be good."

They waited, hearing the car stop below and then the tap of footsteps up the echoing staircase. A key scraped in the lock. They were standing shoulder to shoulder as though awaiting an attack when Brigid's mother came in.

Nell Johnson was a slim woman with high cheekbones, long fingers, and ankles which might have been described as bony if they had not been so fine. During her schooldays Brigid had envied her mother — those grisly speech-days when she had felt so lumpy in her chocolate-coloured uniform and Nell had looked so cool and confident and so much smarter than the other mothers! — and she still envied her. Nell's hair had gone grey early, but even this had proved to be an asset. The two shades of iron were so sharply defined in narrow streaks across her head that jealous friends often asked where she managed to get such skilful tinting done.

Now she kissed Brigid and turned her cheek for Martin to give it a ritual peck.

She said: "You're still set on having that deep blue carpet for the bedroom?"

Discussing the matter at home last night, Brigid had been almost persuaded that the subject should be opened again with Martin. Now, glancing at him, she knew that it simply had to be the deep blue carpet.

"Yes," she said.

"But I thought . . . "

"Deep blue," said Brigid shortly.

"All right, dear." said Nell. "No need

to snap at me." Her voice went up a few tones, as it invariably did when she wanted to establish a rapport with Martin. "We can see who's going to make the decisions in *this* house if we're not careful, can't we? I hope you're prepared to be firm, Martin."

"When necessary." He managed a smile.

"Oh, it'll be necessary. You may not have seen Brigid's temper yet, but you will. Dear me, you will. Have I told you about the time we put a new picture up in her room — when she was only five — and just because we hadn't consulted her . . . "

"Yes, Mummy," said Brigid, "you *have* told him. At least three times."

Nell shrugged. "Oh, well." She had come in carrying a bulky brown envelope. Now she opened it and took out a swatch of material. "If you're having the green carpet in this room . . . "

"That's fixed, too," said Brigid tensely.

"So I understood. And when I saw this curtain material, I felt you ought to have a look at it." She held it up to the light. "Don't you think it would go beautifully?"

Martin moved casually away down the room, back to the window overlooking the demolition site.

The material was mottled green, sprinkled with uneven black blobs. The essence of the pattern was its very lack of pattern. Brigid knew that they would be able to live with it.

"Just right," she admitted.

Nell raised one brindled eyebrow in the direction of Martin. She was silently asking if they had to wait for his approval. When he did not respond she looked round the room. It was surely the twentieth time — or the hundredth? — that she had studied this room. Fond as Brigid was of her mother, she began to share Martin's alarm. She didn't want Nell to impose herself on this flat, any more than she wanted Martin's mother to move in and run it for them. They would sooner make their own mistakes. Better to solve problems themselves and to flounder through the difficulties than to have everything solved for them. It could be fun. Even if it wasn't, the flat would be theirs and the problems and solutions theirs.

"If I were you . . . " Nell caught Brigid's eyes and stopped. She hesitated, then tapped down the room towards Martin, her high heels twitching a dozen echoes into being and losing them in a fraction of a second. She stood beside him, anxious to enlist his sympathy and anxious for both of them to relax in each other's company. Her eyes followed the direction of his gaze. She said: "It's frightening how quickly a century can be wiped out, isn't it? All those people who lived there — all gone."

Martin's wry, appreciative smile was an unexpected response. She had struck the right note.

"All their memories gone, too," he said. "No ghosts. No echoes."

"Just as well, perhaps. I think that house held some unhappy echoes."

Brigid joined them at the window. The gaping hole of the cellar seemed larger. Another section had been exposed to the sky, and on the far side of the fire the men were clearing another heap of rubble away. It was hard to believe that this ravaged patch of land could ever provide a level base for a new building.

16

"Some local scandal?" Brigid asked idly.

"One that we were involved in, actually. Well . . . your grandfather, anyway. Before the first world war. The firm used to be Blythe and Johnson then. That was the Blythe house — that mess over there. Blythe cleared out — something shady, I think — and his name was dropped from the firm. I know your father was always being told by *his* father how hard he'd have to get the company back on its feet." Nell held the curtain material up again and picked abstractedly at it with a fingernail. "Whatever it was," she said, "it was all over long ago."

A workman on the crumbling edge of the cellar waved across the site and shouted something. Two of his mates scrambled over the rubble and stood beside him. Smoke from the fire obscured them for a moment but when it had drifted away they were still standing there. Another man joined them and leaned on his pick. They might have been contemplating a hole in the road, philosophising about it.

"A good job your father can't see

them," said Nell. "That's how they earn their money nowadays — watching faces in the fire."

"Maybe they've discovered some Roman remains," Martin suggested.

The remains which the workmen had discovered belonged in fact to a much more recent period of history. Interred in a corner of the cellar was the fully-clothed corpse of a man dressed in clothes of Edwardian cut. The burial had elements of an ancient religious rite about it, since what was left of the body was accompanied by two suitcases packed with further clothes and personal belongings, as though for use on the man's journey through the next world. They were, however, less impressive than the rich contents of a Egyptian tomb: the only items of any grandeur were a pair of silver-backed hairbrushes and two pairs of gold cuff-links.

All over long ago, Nell had said as she looked at the shell of the Blythe house. She had chosen an unfortunate time for her pronouncement.

The deductions of the forensic experts

and the identifiable contents of the suitcase left little doubt that the corpse was that of Walter Blythe, who had vanished in 1913. It was presumed then that he had fled the country. Certainly somebody appeared to have packed his bags for him; but he had not left. He had died — and it had not been a natural death. It seemed reasonable to suppose that whoever had been responsible for laying him in such an unorthodox grave had also been responsible for savagely battering in his skull.

2

THE door and telephone bells had been ringing in violent spasms for a day and a half. Nell, Arthur, Brigid and the maid shared out defence duties in their besieged fortress. The maid answered the door, got rid of such reporters and busybodies as she could, and called for Brigid when the assault grew too insistent. Nell dealt with the telephone, saying firmly that her husband was busy, could not be disturbed, and had no statement to make. Only when the caller grew abusive did she pass him on to Arthur. They all four used non-committal phrases like blunt weapons, intent only on keeping attackers at a proper distance; but by the end of the first day Nell began to feel that it would not take her long to abandon a purely defensive role and grow vicious.

Murder by person or persons unknown: that had been the coroner's unsurprising verdict. It left the people of Lurgate and the Press plenty of scope for speculation. Two reporters from national dailies and one from a lurid Sunday newspaper came to stay at local hotels. From the intensity of their attack on the Johnson household it was easy to deduce that they had been given only a day or two in which to produce dramatic stories. The current international crisis was no more exciting than the last one had been, and there was space to spare for a juicy mystery, even if it did stem from a killing more than fifty years ago. There was in fact more room for conjecture and less likelihood of any awkward legal actions than if the murder had been a contemporary one. But results had to be quick and colourful or the whole thing would be dropped.

"If we sit tight," said Arthur, "it'll blow over. Stand by to repel boarders, and wait for sundown."

He sounded reassuring but Nell saw that he was hard hit. The reporters would go away when they saw that there was nothing to be gained by staying. This was no big story and could never be inflated into one. The Easter road deaths would

21

be along very shortly, and at least twice in the coming month the Prime Minister could be relied on to do or say something stupid enough to warrant a front-page spread. But locally the matter would not be so easily forgotten. A large number of the telephone calls had been from devoted friends who wouldn't dream of mentioning the murder but who somehow steered the conversation that way and sympathetically wondered what Arthur Johnson was going to do.

What was there for him to do? Nell wanted to shout at them, to din into their stupid heads that Arthur had not even been born when Walter Blythe died. It had nothing to do with him; couldn't possibly be supposed to affect him in any way: yet it did affect him and they both knew it and neither of them knew what they could do about it.

By the late afternoon of the second day friends and reporters had slackened in their attentions. Brigid wanted to go for a walk and meet Martin on his way back from the research centre, and Nell agreed they ought to be able to cope without her. When she crossed the hall with Brigid she felt that she was escorting her through enemy lines. A volley of fire might meet them as they opened the front door. Her nerves prickled and her arms were stinging as though she had been out in a harsh sun or had drunk too much coffee. It was absurd, but she was ready to believe that Brigid was liable to walk into an ambush. She would be captured and held until she talked.

And there was nothing to talk about. That was what was most frustrating of all. There was nothing they could say.

"Don't worry." Brigid squeezed her arm. "I'll be quite safe. Nobody's committed any crime — not in this generation' anyway."

Nell winced. "You think what everyone else thinks, then?"

"I don't know what to think. Mummy, I didn't . . . "

"It's all right. I just feel all of a twitch. It'll pass. You run along."

Brigid's hand was reaching for the knob, but it stayed poised and uncertain. Light from the tall window beside the door divided her face, leaving half of it in

23

worried shadow. She was wearing a plum-coloured sweater and black slacks, with a plum-and-blue band to keep her hair back. The light glowed in her crisp brown curls — an overlapping and interweaving of hair which Nell envied but which exasperated Brigid because there was no way of disciplining the curls into any other style. She touched the door but did not turn the knob. Her fingers were long like her mother's; she had her father's deep, warm eyes. In the past there had been the inevitable dispute as to which side of the family she 'belonged' to. Arthur and Nell were only too glad to concede that she was Brigid in her own right.

She said anxiously: "You're sure you'll be all right? If you want me to stay, I can easily ring Martin."

"He'll be on his way by now. Don't keep him waiting."

"He'll guess why I've been held up. Either he'll come round or he'll phone."

She was aching to go and meet Martin, but Nell knew that one word would have been enough to bring her hand away from that door. It was good to be so sure of her.

24

In a few weeks' time all that Brigid was would belong to Martin Hemming. It was impossible not to think of it in those terms. Martin was going to take her away from them. Nell hoped he was good enough for Brigid. It was an old-fashioned, out moded, ridiculous way of thinking. The phrase itself was embarrassingly out of date. Yet all she could hope was that Martin was good enough for her daughter.

She had never been sure of Martin. It was not that she accused him, even in her own mind, of scheming to marry money: his feelings for Brigid were too obviously sincere. But had they been so at the start? His mother was a fanatic about her only son and, doting on him since his father's death, could have nudged him towards Brigid. Quite a catch.

Brigid said tentatively: "Well, if you're sure . . ."

"Of course I'm sure. Go on, now."

Brigid opened the door just as the bell rang. It shocked them both on to the defensive. Nell advanced a few determined steps. If another reporter was waiting outside she had every intention

25

of driving him away by physical force if necessary.

Slowly Brigid pulled the door right back.

They both sighed explosively.

On the step stood Henry Kersfield, Arthur's solicitor. Beside him was an elderly man with a chalky face and puffy loops of flesh under his eyes. At the sight of Nell he half bowed with a creaky, old-world courtliness.

"Hello, Nell. Here we are. Bang on time. Right on the dot." Kersfield liked to spit his remarks out in short bursts. Nell suspected that his favourite Mitty-ish fantasy was one in which he had been transformed into a famous barrister who demolished one witness after another with swift, unerring barbs. Conversation with him was difficult because his decisiveness made every least little comment sound harsh and final. "All ready for the post mortem? If I may put it that way. All set."

"Arthur's expecting you?"

"He didn't tell you? Phoned me an hour ago."

Lucky we hadn't got outposts stationed

to shoot you down, thought Nell. Aloud she said: "It's been rather a day. Do come in."

The two men came in as Brigid began to slide round the door and out of the house. Kersfield slapped her amiably on the shoulder in passing.

"Meeting the victim? Condemned couple eating a hearty supper — candlelight, soft music? Make the most of it."

"We're going for a walk," said Brigid.

"He's taking you on a mystery tour? Watch it, my dear."

"I've already decided where we're going."

"You have? Wearing the trousers already!"

Brigid went down the drive. Nell closed the door by inches, watching. Nobody sprang out of the bushes and gave chase.

She turned back to their guests.

"Need a strong young man to stand up to that girl of yours," said Kersfield breezily.

Last week Nell had worried about just that point. Now there were other things to worry about. She looked at the older man. Kersfield took his cue.

"Don't think you know Mr Farnham, Nell. Mr Farnham — Mrs Johnson."

The old man's hand was leathery and incredibly cold.

"Farnham?" Nell smiled, and waited for the sound of the name to strike a resonance. Then she got it. "Oh. You're the Mr Farnham of Farnham, Farnham and Kersfield."

"The middle one." The pouchy eyes blinked heavily at her. "I expect you thought I was dead."

"Oh, I . . ."

"Sometimes I'm not sure I'm not."

Arthur came out of his study and approached them. Kersfield made the introductions again.

"Mr Farnham handled a lot of your father's work in his time. And Blythe's. Knew them both well. It struck me he could fill in any details. Though I've got most of them taped. Between us we can settle it all tonight, I think. Right?"

"I'll leave you to it," said Nell, turning away.

"No, you won't," said Arthur quietly. He smiled at his visitors. "No secrets from my wife. She'd insist on my telling

28

her all about it afterwards, so she may as well sit in with us. That way I'll save my breath."

His flippancy hid neither a command nor an appeal for support. In twenty-five years of marriage the two of them had shared everything and he simply wanted her to share this.

They went into the study.

Arthur pulled chairs to the front of his desk. He would have been uncomfortable sitting behind the desk like a tycoon presiding over a meeting.

This was not really a study. It was the equivalent of a boy's den. Here Arthur liked to relax from time to time with his treasures. Here he could slacken off his characteristic briskness and efficiency; could be most at ease. The fact that Nell could come in and out as she pleased was the most loving compliment he could have paid her.

There were plans and photographs of historic buildings all over the walls. A litter of sketches curled over the flat top of the map cabinet. It was understood that this room was never to be tidied. Systematic and meticulous elsewhere, in this room Arthur was in his mental shirt-sleeves.

His father had expected him to carry on the family tradition in the firm and loyally he had done so. There were times when he felt constricted in Lurgate and longed to break out and work on new schemes in new places. Instead, he applied himself all the more doggedly to his own neighbourhood, preserving what was good in the old Lurgate and helping to create what was new and necessary. Preservation was as important as replacement. He became an acknowledged expert who could be summoned to the far side of the county if there was news of some historic building in danger, some threat by slap-dash planners to fine architecture which was not sufficiently protected from vandals — vandals, he would emphasise, in the same profession as himself. He gave advice on preservation and careful reconstruction free and freely.

This side of the house was in shadow. Arthur switched on his desk lamp. The bald front of his head shone in the light. This high bald crown, fringed at the back with a boyishly dishevelled mop of jet-black hair, was sunburnt or at least weatherbeaten most of the year. Apart from his liking for this scrap-book of a room, he was not an indoor man. He wanted to be where the work was being done, and most of his life was spent in the open.

He offered a cigarette box around and said: "You've gone into it thoroughly?"

"Sleepless night, Arthur. Pretty well sleepless. Closed the doors, kept everybody out, and dug up the lot. Dislodged a lot of dust, let me tell you. I never thought," said Kersfield, "we'd have to dig up the name of Blythe again."

It was not, thought Nell, the happiest way of putting it.

The firm of Blythe and Johnson, building contractors, had been established in the first decade of the century. Walter Blythe, the older of the two partners, was a volatile, exuberant man who saw how to exploit opportunities when they existed and how to create opportunities where none had existed before. Victor Johnson was more thoughtful and more meticulous: his friend provided the steam but it was Victor who kept things on the rails and kept them moving along those rails.

Lurgate in 1905 was a small town whose main livelihood came from fishing. But prosperity was leading more and more people to take holidays by the sea. The fashionable resorts were faced with the rivalry of smaller towns not too far from London yet not too close to the city. The railways spun a web over Kent and Sussex. The three hills on which Lurgate was built were little more than hummocks but they provided a picturesque background and, by huddling round the sandy bay, protected it from wind on all save the most blustery winter days. The place was, as a later generation might put it, ripe for development.

Blythe and Johnson built a terrace of tall houses facing the sea. A couple were taken at once by well-to-do gentlemen with large families and ailing wives for whom sea air had been prescribed. The others became good-class boarding-houses. Blythe and Johnson built hotels, shops to cater to the summer influx of visitors, and whole streets of small houses up and over the hills. The fishing quarter of the town became a picturesque feature for the visitors but continued as a working entity. The fishermen dourly watched the white buildings go up until they formed a rampart commanding the sea from every available acre of ground, and the native community became in fact more tightly knit than ever before. Holidaymakers were foreigners. You might make more money taking these folk on trips round the headland out to sea than you could from fishing, but you never really mixed with them or accepted them. Come the first cold breezes of the autumn and they were away. Then the new streets looked bare and useless but the old town was still the old town.

Blythe and Johnson prospered. The two men worked well as a team. "Though I wouldn't have said they had the same ideas at all," observed old Mr Farnham. "Walter Blythe was always one for putting on a big show. He had to have the biggest house — had it built for himself when the firm really ought to have been concentrating on selling to other people. And when motor-cars came in of course he had to have one and smell up the countryside with it. A fair terror he was. Oh, and his wife — she had to be special, too. He couldn't just marry a local girl. He had to do something spectacular. One year he came back from holiday and announced he was going to marry a foreign girl, and a few weeks later she arrived and they had a big splash."

"Foreign?" Nell smiled despite herself. "You mean the girl came from more than five miles outside Lurgate?"

"Oh, further than that. She was really foreign. Very dark. Very beautiful, I suppose. But she wasn't well liked. She thought far too much of herself, and of course Walter Blythe encouraged her. The folk here didn't have much time for her."

"Poor girl."

"Victor Johnson, now — your father, Mr Johnson — he was a worker. He drove his men and he was a real scourge to any sub-contractors they had to take on. But he drove himself, too. We always reckoned that Blythe had the great ideas but it was up to Johnson to make them work. And when we saw Blythe driving round the countryside, and sometimes out with some girl he had no business to be out with, some of us said Johnson made the money so that Blythe could spend it."

"My father was a strict man," Arthur nodded. "He wanted things done straight. He was generous enough, but he hated waste."

"We often wondered if there'd come a time when he'd have to put his foot down."

"And did there?"

"Well . . . " Mr Farnham coughed apologetically. "It does look like it, doesn't it?"

Arthur appeared hot and tired although it was cool in this room. Nell wanted to move her chair closer to his and sit beside him. He was wretched and she wanted to be near him.

Henry Kersfield took over, dry and analytical, from Mr Farnham. He wished it to be understood that he was dealing with blunt facts rather than reminiscence and vague generalisation.

In 1913 Walter Blythe disappeared. He went overnight, without warning. His partner, Victor Johnson, expressed surprise. So did the dark, imperious Mrs Blythe. Her husband had said nothing to her about going on a trip. Yet she confirmed that he had taken plenty of luggage.

"Nobody cared for her," Mr Farnham broke in, "but you had to be sorry for her. She was too proud for her own good; but that pride of hers must have had a nasty blow when she was left like that."

"Your father," Kersfield said to Arthur, "called the firm's accountant in. They went through the books together and announced that ten thousand pounds were missing. It was a lot of money in those days. It was certainly a lot so far as Blythe and Johnson were concerned. The supposition at the time was that Blythe had converted the embezzled money to negotiable securities. Could even have loaded himself with sovereigns — quite feasible then. Anyway, the money was gone, Blythe was gone. Off to South America, everybody thought."

"Why South America?" asked Nell.

Mr Farnham smiled nostalgically. "It was always South America in those days."

The firm was almost crippled by the

loss. Victor Johnson grimly refused to be beaten. It was known to everyone in Lurgate that he devoted every minute of his waking life to building things up again. Blythe and Johnson became Johnson and Son. Victor died in his middle fifties and Nell remembered very little about him: she had married Arthur in 1941, when both of them had been in the Services, and met Arthur's father once on a ten days' leave and once on a forty-eight-hour pass. His wife had died years before and his only interests in life were the firm and his son — interests which blended and became inextricably one. To Nell he was brusque but charming, but he was already a sick, tired man and she did not know him long enough to be taken into his confidence on anything that mattered to him.

Arthur told her that during his adolescence his father had often come out with snippets of information about the difficult years of rebuilding, usually as an illustration to some precept about hard work and honesty. By that time the details of the past had perhaps grown hazy, or perhaps Victor Johnson didn't wish to be too explicit. To Arthur, Walter Blythe was no more than a dim figure on the far side of an earlier war, in a world lost beyond recall. When his father died, a year after Arthur and Nell were married, there was no-one to remember Blythe.

Nell said: "Did he . . . did Mr Johnson do anything about Mrs Blythe?"

Mr Farnham remembered this very well. He had been a young partner in the firm then, and had been present at a meeting which his father had set up. There must have been an earlier, private meeting when Victor Johnson and possibly his wife had talked to Mrs Blythe. After all, the two married couples were close friends — the men working together, the wives spending a lot of time together in the absence of their husbands.

Victor had been a puritan and was outraged by his partner's dishonesty. But Mrs Johnson must have prevailed on him to be charitable towards Mrs Blythe, equally badly treated. Mr Farnham was sure that she was the one who suggested that Mrs Blythe should be given an allowance. It was unfair that the poor young woman should suffer because of her husband's defection.

In fact Mrs Blythe refused to accept a penny. She was too proud.

"Very fiery about it," said Mr Farnham. "She cursed her husband in some outlandish language. And she thanked the Johnsons and said she wouldn't touch what was left of the money."

"But how did she manage?" asked Nell. She could not bear to think of the misery of a girl deserted by her husband in a land that was alien to her.

But she hadn't been deserted. That was only how it had seemed at the time.

And that was how it had seemed to Mrs Blythe. It must have been real enough and ghastly enough at the time.

Kersfield said: "She did her own vanishing trick. Ten days later. Just like Walter Blythe — no trace of her."

"And naturally," said Mr Farnham, reliving old gossip and old emotions, "we took it for granted that she'd gone to join Blythe."

"In South America?"

"In South America. Living on his ill-gotten gains. The Johnsons were relieved they hadn't actually given Mrs Blythe any money, since she was obviously, after all, a party to the whole swindle. Once Blythe was safely away, he sent for her and she went to join him. That," said Mr Farnham heavily, "was how it appeared at the time."

"And now . . . "

"Now," said Kersfield, "we're faced with the fact that Blythe never left the country. He was murdered." He almost sparkled with glee at an idea which had just occurred to him, then assumed a suitably grave expression. "One wonders. One does indeed. One wonders if there's a possibility of Mrs Blythe's corpse turning up also."

Nell had a vision of a woman's body with a couple of bags packed beside it in the same gruesome way. The Blythe house might have further hideous revelations to yield up. She turned supplicatingly to Arthur. He said to Kersfield:

"The whole cellar has been torn out by now. There's nothing else there."

"Might be somewhere else."

"It seems much more likely that Mrs Blythe disappeared of her own accord," said Arthur. "We've been told she was very proud ... "

"Impetuous, too." Mr Farnham was glad to resume his role of expert on the parties concerned. "She would fly off the handle at the least little thing. No, it's simple enough. Mr Johnson's right. She wasn't going to take charity from the Johnsons and she wasn't going to hang around in Lurgate as an object of pity or shame."

The image of the packed cases remained obstinately in Nell's mind. She said: "Supposing Blythe was in fact the embezzler he's always been thought, and he was about to make a getaway when Arthur's father caught him?"

"And killed him?" Kersfield shrugged. "Doesn't make it any better for Johnson. The late Mr Johnson, I mean. Murder's still murder. And how would that fit in with Mrs Blythe's behaviour? If she'd been in it with Blythe, she'd be waiting to clear out with him and the money. If he disappeared mysteriously, she'd raise hell to find him. She'd soon have been on to Johnson. But if she didn't know — if he was planning to leave without her, then ... " He blinked, sorting out the

41

permutations. There were some things that short, blustering sentences wouldn't solve. "Yes, of course. If she *didn't* know, then she could have been expected to do exactly what she did: she ran away in the belief that he had deserted her. Humiliated her. She just wanted to turn her back on the whole place. Back to our original premise."

All theories were of equal weight because there was no way of checking any of them. Nell saw no reason why she shouldn't contribute. She said:

"We can't be sure it wasn't Mrs Blythe who killed her husband."

She was ashamed to clutch at such a straw. She was accusing someone who couldn't answer back. But in this at least the dead were on the same footing: none of them could answer the questions of the living.

Kersfield said: "Can't see why Mrs Blythe should want to get rid of her husband. Prosperous — gave her everything she asked for. And how could she have tampered with the books on her own? Very skilful tampering, I assure you we've gone through them with your own accountant. The embezzlement was carried out by someone who knew the firm's operations back to front. We've always assumed it was Blythe, and of course he wasn't there to supply a plausible explanation."

"And my father was," said Arthur quietly.

Nell could feel within herself how this must be hurting him. He had accepted his father's sternly reiterated principles and had uncomplainingly accepted his father's assumption that he would keep the name of Johnson alive in the firm. Now he had to face the terrible likelihood of his father's severe integrity having been a protracted bluff, a whole way of life built on hypocrisy.

"I'm afraid," said Kersfield, "that the story which fits best is the most distasteful one. Sorry, Arthur. Your father could have cooked the books in such a way as to throw blame on his partner. Everything pointing to an embezzlement. He must have come and gone pretty freely in the Blythe household. Easy enough to remove clothes and pack suitcases. Make it look as though Blythe had beaten it with plenty of his

43

belongings. Calculated flight — not just a mysterious disappearance which might have led to suspicions of foul play."

"But why? Why should my father have gone mad like that? Because that's what it was — mad. He was a very strict man. Strict, moral, honest. Almost too much so."

"Precisely," said Kersfield. "Almost too much so. Couldn't that be the explanation? We've heard from Mr Farnham that Blythe was a spendthrift. Perhaps it was getting out of hand. He gallivanted around too much. I think that's what they called it in those days."

"Gallivanted," said Mr Farnham. "Yes. Oh, yes, he did.

"Johnson had to do the work while Blythe squandered the profits. Your father was a fanatic when it came to work — building the place up, keeping it on its feet. And who stood in his way? Who drove him to distraction by never taking things seriously? His pleasure-loving partner."

Nell looked at Arthur. He was sunk in contemplation of his desk. He must be reviewing yet again the history of his father's lectures to him, the exhortations, the tales of struggle and achievement. If Victor Johnson had murdered Walter Blythe, what had happened to the missing money? Had it really never been missing at all? Had there been no struggle to keep the firm going? The firm of Johnson and Son, minus the name of Blythe, had been a success in the end. Had it in fact been a cunningly organised success all along?

They had been talking about Mrs Blythe's injured pride. Nell wondered if these two men realised just how Arthur's family pride must be suffering now.

And the personal ambitions he had given up in order to fulfil his father's wishes, even after his father's death — had the sacrifice been wasted?

"The legal situation" — Kersfield decided it was time to sum up — "is that you can't be blamed for anything. Not possibly. It's old history. The principals are dead. It's doubtful whether anyone can ever sort out who killed Walter Blythe. And even if they could, it'd be difficult to establish any claim against you. No questions of inheritance arise. If Blythe had had any children, there might of course be some awkward moral issues . . . "

"None," said Mr Farnham. "She was a fine figure of a woman, Mrs Blythe — just the type, one would have thought — but there weren't any children."

"As we say in court," said Kersfield, "there's no case to answer."

No case to answer, thought Nell. And because no case could ever be brought, there could never be a verdict. No verdict of guilty — but no acquittal.

"Very distressing for you," said Kersfield. "I can imagine how you must feel, Arthur." But he couldn't, thought Nell. How could he possibly imagine? "Don't let it get you down," he said. "No-one can blame you. All happened before either of you was born. No blame at all — legal or moral. That's my professional opinion."

But someone had to be blamed. Nell knew that. In a community like Lurgate the local faces had long memories. Those memories had been happily shaken up and turned out into the daylight recently. You were held to be in some way mystically responsible for who your ancestors were and what they did.

The telephone rang. Nell began to get out of her chair to intercept the call. Arthur was there before her.

"Johnson. Mm? Yes ... Look, I've answered these questions God knows how many times already ... What?"

Kersfield leaned forward and put out his hand. "If that's a reporter, let me ... "

But Arthur was already speaking. "Yes, you may print that. You may say I accept no legal responsibility for events which took place half a century ago, but that if there should be any descendants or relatives of Walter Blythe alive today and in need, I'll be glad to hear from them."

Kersfield let out a little squeak and shook his head. "Shouldn't have said that," he whispered to Nell. "Every crank in the country, you know — all be writing to him. Should have left it to me. Absolutely no call for that statement."

But Nell knew that it was the only way in which Arthur could possibly have reacted. He was used to making decisions without long conferences. He had made his decision now. Putting the receiver down, he gave Kersfield no chance to

47

utter a formal protest.

"I can't bear fuzzy edges. Let's have everything clear and settled. Out in the open."

If only it could be like that, thought Nell: out in the open.

Murder by person or persons unknown.

Plenty of fuzzy edges there. But it was settled in the minds of everyone in Lurgate who the 'person unknown' must have been. The Johnsons were going to have to live with that unuttered, unanswerable accusation.

3

BRIGID felt rather than heard the silent murmurs as she walked one Sunday afternoon towards Martin's home.

The park was like an aviary, alive with chatter. Children hopped and skipped from the grass on to the paths as Brigid took the diagonal route to the far gate. They didn't care about her: they stumbled round her or bumped into her, laughed as they hurried off, and went on with their games. It was the mothers and grandmothers who, here and there, turned heads to follow her progress. A woman she knew smiled at her. A woman she didn't know smiled to herself.

By the nineteen-sixties three main elements were clearly identifiable in Lurgate. The core of local families remained, but the sons and daughters of fishermen had turned more and more towards the running of boarding-houses and cafés and gift shops, and the grandsons who had not emigrated to London tended to travel to Maidstone or Canterbury for better-paid jobs. Nevertheless they went on thinking of themselves as the real Lurgate people. Then there was a sector of white-collar commuters who had bought property here because it was cheaper than in London and the climate was so good for the children. The third element was supplied by the tourists and trippers, bringing money into the town at Easter and Whitsun and taking it over completely during the summer months. The locals fished, made profits from the visitors, and complained about the visitors. Businessmen and the visitors between them inspired the laying out of a golf course and just managed to keep the cinema going. The businessmen used the town's amenities all year round and felt that their contribution was what really kept the place alive. Most of the holidaymakers felt, without consciously putting it in such naive terms, that Lurgate went into suspended animation for that part of the year when they were absent.

News of the discovery of Walter Blythe's

remains affected them all in different ways. The commuters read of it on the morning train with an odd gratification. In some way it stimulated their local pride. Lurgate was in the news. Some of them had bought houses built by Johnson's but for most of them the name was merely one that appeared on boards at the edge of building sites. Now the name, the firm and the town had acquired a brief notoriety and, more substantially, a history. The newspapers carried the same story to London, the Midlands and the North. A few hundred men said to their wives: "Look at this — remember our fortnight in Lurgate?" And in the factory or office they mentioned with satisfaction that they had been in Lurgate last year and were actually going again this year.

The inbred memories of the older residents had been coaxed out into the light of day by reporters and, once out, proceeded to multiply. Old stories were revived. Men and women in their late fifties suddenly found that they had vivid recollections of Walter Blythe. They had seen him in the street; he used to pass their house every day, regular as clockwork; he used to buy their fathers a drink every Saturday — got on very well with Dad, he did. Younger people dug up details which their parents had told them; older ones who had really known Walter basked in the deference which was accorded them for a while. Old rumours became hard facts. Arguments grew acrimonious.

"That wife of his — if you was to dig deep enough, you'd find something *there*, if you ask me . . . "

"Italian, she was."

"No, she was Spanish. Very dark. Spoke Spanish when she got excited, like."

"Of course she was dark. That's because she was Italian. I can hear her voice like it was yesterday."

"Touch of the tarbrush, I'd say."

"Didn't have no time for anyone. Didn't half fancy herself, that gel."

Brigid was shocked by the exhibition of naked delight. It was as though the people of Lurgate had been maliciously waiting for years for the chance to belittle the Johnsons.

There was a small rash of meaningless telephone calls. Most of them were incoherent, one or two obscene. They were all anonymous.

After her father's announcement that he would be prepared to help any existing relatives of Walter Blythe 'restitution' was a word used by one newspaperman — there came a flood of letters and several visitors to the house. They were all pitifully untruthful and transparent. Two or three charitable organisations rushed appeals through the post as though the Johnsons had won a football pool and might be persuaded to distribute some of their winnings. Arthur Johnson bore it unflinchingly but a disquieting greyness crept under his normal healthy brown. He spent more time at home than on his various building sites. When he went out on a tour of inspection Brigid and her mother could see how tense he was, dreading the mute appraisal of his employees and anyone else he might meet during the day.

My grandfather was a murderer, said Brigid to herself. She waited for some reaction; and there was none. It meant nothing. She had never known her grandfather. It meant more to the people around her than it did to her — the people who had nothing better to occupy their time than picking over the decayed remnants of a dead scandal.

The promenade narrowed as it approached the bluff. Here at the end of the promontory were only sea, sky, the cliff face and the smooth paving. Grey and bleak in winter, the surface of the promenade hurt the eyes during days of sunshine. As Brigid turned the corner, wind off the sea ruffled her hair.

High on the slope above, Fernrock Hotel's windows stared out over the water. The rooms where Martin and his mother lived were invisible from this angle. They were at the side, close to the hedge which marked the edge of the terraced gardens. A road along the crown of the ridge led to the hotel's main entrance. From the sea road one had a choice of routes: there were two flights of uncompromisingly direct steps, or a winding path lined by shrubs. The bushes and trees on the terraces all leaned away from the prevailing wind at such a uniform angle that they made the hotel itself appear to tilt in the opposite direction.

Brigid struck impatiently up the nearest steep flight of steps.

Every Sunday she came for tea with Martin and his mother. She supposed they would have to maintain this ritual after they were married. And they would have to invite Mrs Hemming to their flat. And her own mother and father. Already there seemed to be an awful lot of obligations piling up. What if they didn't *want* to see anyone else for a week on end?

Martin had seen her coming and was waiting on the hotel steps.

"Mother's dealing with a complaint about a bathroom on the third floor. She'll be down in a few minutes."

They walked along the level stretch of grass below the main windows. Out on the skyline a tanker hung apparently motionless while blobs of cloud out-distanced it. Three blue sails twisted and darted past the end of the bluff and across the bay.

Martin's hand gripped her arm and slowed her. "Careful."

A few yards away the orderly pattern of the terraces was broken. A small fissure in the ground ran from the windbreak of trees beside the hotel, widening until it formed a great gash. The flowerbeds at the foot of the slope had collapsed into the miniature abyss.

"We didn't have an earthquake last night, did we?" said Brigid. "Or was it just one of your guests, throwing one of your home-made cakes out of the window?"

"Better not let Mum hear you say that."

They approached the edge of the gash. It was not deep, but the raggedness of the splintered stone gave it the appearance of an ugly wound. Brigid thoughtfully prodded a lump of soil forward with her foot and watched it separate and trickle down a few inches of raw, newly exposed rock. She shivered. It was as bad as forcing dirt into scratched, bleeding flesh.

She said: "This isn't going to get any worse, is it?"

"We hope not. Don't want our only capital to disappear into the earth."

56

"Faults are always opening up along the coast. They don't usually split more than a few inches."

"Don't breathe on it, anyway," said Martin. "Come away."

He took her hand and coaxed her away. They kissed. When their lips were parted and close together, the breeze whistled faintly between them. They laughed and turned to face the sea, so that the wind played a moaning tune through their teeth.

"How's your mother?" asked Brigid.

It was a formality. She asked the question in the expectation of his saying, "All right." Then they could go on to talk about themselves. And Martin said, "All right" — but with an intonation that alerted her at once.

She said: "What's wrong?"

"Nothing. Nothing at all."

"Has something happened?"

"Nothing. She's all right."

"Is she worried about that crack in the cliff?"

He sounded relieved, glad to take advantage of this. "You know how she fusses over every little thing."

Brigid said: "It *is* only that, is it?"

"What else could there be?"

She wasn't going to nag. That was something she had promised herself, and it was one of her unspoken promises to Martin. When they were married she wouldn't nag and fidget and go on at him. Not about anything at all. And if she wasn't going to do it when they were married, she mustn't do it now. But she was upset. There was something he wasn't telling her. So far she had never been aware of his keeping any secrets from her or avoiding any questions.

Mrs Hemming came round the corner of the hotel.

"Do you want tea, or don't you?"

They went in.

The table in the small sitting room was laid with a glittering white cloth whose ironed folds stood up in small ridges. A large fruit cake stood on a plate at the intersection of the main folds.

"One of yours?" said Brigid appreciatively.

"Hm. One of my failures."

"It looks lovely."

"It's a mess," said Mrs Hemming unequivocally.

She was a lean woman with sinewy arms and rough, hardskinned hands. She worked relentlessly and found it hard to talk casually with people who lived different lives from her own. Since the death of her husband in the Korean war she had run the Fernrock Hotel and brought up Martin without help and without complaint. The only subject on which she ever expressed resentment was her husband's death and even then there was a flourish of contempt for those who hadn't suffered as she had. "He ought never to have gone. He didn't have to. He could easily have got out of it, at his age. But he wouldn't."

The problems of the hotel and the hundreds of guests who had passed through it over the years had fostered in her a brusque manner that was not so much aggressive as half-challenging: she could let nothing pass unobserved, could not restrain forthright comments when she felt they were deserved, and was incapable of abandoning herself to the pleasures of purely idle conversation. She expected things to go wrong somewhere whenever her back was turned, and was sure — not without reason — that none but herself could be trusted to put them right. Brigid had grown to like her because she was Martin's mother, because she had such bright grey eyes whose shyness was not often appreciated by others, and because of something honest and appealing in her very awkwardness. Yet each time she came here she also felt afraid. There was always an odd feeling that Mrs Hemming might turn on her and repudiate her.

They started with salmon and cucumber sandwiches, and ate for a while in silence. Martin essayed a smile at Brigid and she knew there was something wrong with it. A minute later she observed that he was glancing at his mother; and Mrs Hemming was resolutely looking at her plate.

Brigid said: "Martin was showing me that fault in the cliff, right through your garden."

"Hm."

"After all the trouble you've taken over the terraces — it's a dreadful shame."

"We'll have to fence it off. We don't want people falling in." Mrs Hemming sounded as though nothing would please her better than the sight of people falling in.

They finished the sandwiches and turned their attention to the cake.

"Let's see the worst," said Martin too loudly.

"You'll do that all right." His mother sliced angrily through the cake. "I had to leave the oven to go and calm down some fool of a woman who said she'd had a shock from the fire in her room. Lot of rubbish, of course. And I forgot about the cake, and it's not what it ought to be."

"None of us are," said Martin.

Brigid held her plate out. Mrs Hemming put a large slice of cake on it and still did not look directly at her.

Brigid said: "Plenty of bookings for Easter, I suppose?"

"Hm."

The cake was excellent, but Brigid knew that there would be no point in saying so. She wondered if there had been some sort of argument before she arrived. Something connected with their wedding cake, perhaps — the cake which Mrs Hemming had insisted on making, and about which perhaps she had been as morose and hypercritical as she had been about this fruit cake. Or there might have been a squabble over money. Mrs Hemming was even touchier than Martin on that subject. There had already been one or two outbreaks of bickering over the question of paying for the honeymoon, which Mrs Hemming wanted to take on as her responsibility — though she couldn't for the life of her understand why they wanted to go off to Malta of all places, when there was so little of it and it was such a way away and probably not nearly as healthy as some nice place in Devon or Cornwall.

Brigid turned resolutely to Martin. She could be as stubborn and determined as Mrs Hemming. She *would* break up this weird, brooding atmosphere. She said:

"So they're going to extend the research centre at last."

"We've been yelling for more space for long enough, goodness knows."

"Daddy's been asked to tender. He thinks . . . "

"He can still find time to carry on working, then?" said Mrs Hemming. She glared at a spot halfway between the cake and the edge of her own plate. "It hasn't put him off his stroke, all this?"

Martin's head jerked round. "Mum, you know we agreed . . . "

"It's a fine thing. A fine thing." The words sprayed out as though she were uncontrollably coughing up crumbs. "Only three weeks to the wedding, and now *this*."

"So that's what's been on your mind," said Brigid.

"There's no reason why it should be on *my* mind."

"Then what's all the fuss?" Brigid was curt. She had had enough of the twittering of gossip in the town. She had not expected to encounter such hostility here. And if it was here, she wasn't going to be polite about it.

Mrs Hemming raised her eyes at last, but not in Brigid's direction. She frowned at Martin as she must have frowned when he was a small boy and had done something naughty. "Those new people who arrived this morning. First thing they asked about was the scandal. All the way from Doncaster, and it was the first thing they wanted to know."

"Good for trade." Martin was trying to keep it light. "A much better pull than the pier concert party."

"Hm. I suppose you think we'd get more bookings for the summer if I put out an advertisement saying my son was going to marry the . . . well . . . "

"Well what?" said Martin dangerously, the bantering note gone.

Mrs Hemming dragged Brigid's half-empty teacup towards her and began to splash tea into it. She slopped a yellow stain on to the clean cloth and for once appeared not to notice or not to care.

She had not answered Martin. He said: "What's it got to do with Brigid?"

"I'm not saying it's got anything to do with Brigid."

"Then why are you so cross with me?" asked Brigid. "Why can't you speak to me?"

"I'm not cross with you." Mrs Hemming made a great effort. "I'm sorry. I . . . oh, it's all too awful. I never imagined . . . never . . . "

There was a tap at the door. The porter, an ageless little Lurgate man with leathery features and yellow teeth, peered timidly in.

"Sorry, Mrs H. Those folk just goin' — they'd like a word with you. Some mistake on the bill."

"Mistake?" Mrs Hemming was on her feet immediately. She spared Martin and Brigid a brief nod and then left the room.

She was probably glad to make her escape. Brigid had the impression that she would work off her feelings on the unfortunate porter or even on the departing holidaymakers.

Martin pushed his chair back. "Hell. I'm sorry."

"What's the matter with her?" Brigid demanded. "Why is it so awful? What's it got to do with your mother?"

"Oh, you know how she is."

"No, I don't know how she is. Or I don't understand, anyway. I don't understand why she's so worked up about this."

"Neither do I."

"You'd think she'd been personally insulted in some way."

"I know," said Martin.

"Has she said anything to you?"

"Nothing that makes sense. She's just . . . well, upset. She's always been a bit of a fusspot, bless her." He came round the table to Brigid and bent over her. His right hand slid under her chin and turned her face to his. "You mustn't worry. It's all too stupid. It's something to talk about in the town, that's all."

"And in the hotel, apparently."

"We don't get much like it in Lurgate. Not as meaty as this." He was trying to be flippant, and it wasn't like him. "It'll blow over. A few weeks from now some trippers will smash up the pier pavilion, or a speedboat'll capsize, and they'll all have something else to talk about. This business will die of its own accord."

But it was not yet ready to die. Walter Blythe's ghost, having its fling, was not prepared to lie down so soon.

A few foreign newspapers picked up the story and gave it a few paragraphs. A French illustrated weekly did a feature on mysterious disappearances of the century and wound up with Arthur Johnson's offer to help anyone connected with the

Blythe family who might still be alive. The immediate result was another surge of telephone calls and letters. 'I told you so' was too banal a remark for Kersfield's liking: he conveyed the same message with a shake of the head.

Early one evening Brigid came in from a two-hour session devoted to the fitting of her wedding-dress. Those two hours had convinced her that she undoubtedly had the most awkward proportions ever bestowed on a female of the human species. Amy, the maid, was fidgeting in the hall, obviously on the look-out for her.

"They've been waiting for you, miss. They said you was to go in the minute you got here."

"They?"

"Your mam and dad, miss. There's a young man come."

"Were we expecting a young man?"

"He just rolled up. Asked to see the family." Amy jiggled from one foot to the other. She was a plump, eager little girl, and when she bobbed to and fro it was like the rocking of a stout wooden doll. She had a surprise to spring and wanted to make the most of it. "Said his name was Blythe."

It was like an echo which kept bouncing back off every wall in the town. Most echoes jangled away into nothingness after a while. Not this one.

"Blythe?" said Brigid. "Did he say what . . . who . . . "

"He didn't tell me anything," said Amy regretfully. "But *they* said you was to go in" — she nodded towards the study door — "just as soon as you came in."

4

NELL had expected it to take ten or fifteen minutes at most. Another con trick. Another badly assembled sob story that would fall apart under Arthur's polite but sceptical questioning.

After the first few minutes she began to realise that this one wasn't going to collapse all that easily.

The young man was of medium height, only an inch or two taller than Nell herself. He had dark features and deepest, olive eyes, in startling contrast with his bronze hair. Although he had come into the room with an air of diffidence, there was something calculated about it: even when he was sitting down, lithe and graceful in each smallest movement, there was something predatory about him.

"I am Peter Blythe," he had introduced himself.

The name did not fit his appearance. He was Latin through and through. Yet there was the incongruous hair, and when he spoke it was with only the faintest musical accent.

Arthur settled down to it. "You're a distant relative of the late Walter Blythe?"

The young man smiled a slow, gleaming smile. "I have been distant from England all my life, yes. But I had always known I would come here."

"I mean that your relationship to Walter Blythe . . . "

"I am his grandson."

Nell felt dizzy for a moment. Then her head cleared. This was where the whole business could be wrapped up briefly and conclusively. She waited for Arthur to finish it.

He said: "Walter Blythe had no children, so I don't quite see how he could have had a grandson."

"My grandmother did not know, when she left England, that she was pregnant."

He was quite calm and quite sure of himself. He was not making an appeal and not testing their reactions: he seemed content to state facts and let them do their work.

If these were facts, the young man's

70

moral claim on the firm was considerable.

Arthur said thoughtfully: "This recent discovery must have come as a great surprise to you."

"And to you."

"You'll be able to let us have some credentials — some proof?"

"But of course."

He had brought a narrow, stained briefcase with him and placed it beside his chair. Now he unzipped it and reached in, taking out the first thing which came to hand. He glanced at it, nodded, and passed it to Arthur.

Arthur was sitting behind his desk. It was a useful, formal barrier. Nell walked round it and stood at his shoulder, looking down at the photograph he was examining.

The picture was an old one, with the hard yellow gloss so typical of photographs taken early in the century. It was mounted on a stiff card with deckled edges. Time had perhaps deepened the yellow but it had not blurred the lines of the picture, which showed a young woman with dark hair and very dark eyes standing on a lawn at the back of a house.

Arthur glanced up at her for confirmation. "There's no doubt about the house," said Nell. It was unmistakably the Blythe place.

The young man who called himself Peter Blythe said, unruffled but with a flicker of arrogance: "If you will please make enquiries you will find there is also no doubt about my grandmother."

"How did you come by this?"

"It was with the . . . those things I have from her . . . " He fumbled for a word. "With what she leave me, yes? With . . . "

"Among her effects?" Arthur supplied.

"That is what you say? Yes. Her effects." he lowered his eyes. He had long, feminine eyelashes. "She did not have much to leave me." his voice dropped. His hands opened expressively, then fell sadly to his lap.

Nell was jarred by his self-confidence. The enticing little lilt of his voice and his exaggerated little gestures were embarrassing and out of place; but she was frightened by her own growing belief that behind the emotional mannerisms there lay truth.

More aggressively than she had meant to, she said: "*Peter* Blythe?"

"That is how I was christened. But at home I am usually called Pietro."

"At home?"

"Italy," he said. "Now it is Rome. But when I am a boy it is Sicily, of course. Where my grandmother came from. And where she went back after her husband's disgrace. Or," he said gently, as though not to give offence, "what she believed to be her husband's disgrace."

Arthur handed back the photograph. Peter Blythe dropped it into the brief-case and took out a small sheaf of papers, with the corners of other photographs sticking out. He put them on the desk and delved again. This time he removed a bulge from the brief-case. It proved to be a small travelling clock. He pushed it across the desk, turning it so that Nell and Arthur could see the back.

On it was engraved in a sharp cursive lettering: *Serafina Blythe.*

A recent photograph lay on the top of the pile. It showed what appeared to be signatures in a register.

"Here." The young man's polished nail,

lightly brown as though with nicotine, indicated a line. "The wedding of my mother and father. I made this photograph from the church so that you would see. My father, Luigi Blythe. My mother, Emily Parsons."

"I've no idea what an Italian church register looks like," said Arthur.

"Please check," said the young man amiably.

"Emily Parsons?" said Nell. "Your mother was English, then?"

"My grandmother did not approve. She was very angry. I knew my mother and my grandmother did not love — there was no happiness between them — but it was only when I grew up that I understood why. My grandmother had no reason to love the English, I think? But now we find she was wrong. Her husband did not leave her. Her husband was . . . removed. That is the word — removed?"

Arthur did not reply. He slowly turned over the material on the desk before him. There was a picture of the same young woman, this time holding a baby, taken against a white wall in bright sunlight. There were two frayed envelopes addressed to Mrs Walter Blythe in Lurgate, one of them still containing a folded bill — the sort of scraps that remain among people's belongings for years without ever coming to the surface and being thrown away.

"The other letters," Peter Blythe prompted. He leaned forward and prodded a small batch of letters from the heap. "Please, you read them?"

Arthur unfolded one. "It's a personal letter," he said uncertainly.

"They are all personal. I do not think my grandfather will mind now."

There were two or three brief notes from Walter Blythe to Serafina. He had evidently not been a good letter writer. One had been sent from Florence, presumably to Sicily. Two were rather matter-of-factly amorous scribbles from an address in Scotland. They were the kind of thing a husband away on business would feel he ought to write to his wife at home.

Nell felt as diffident as Arthur when it came to skimming through these letters. They belonged to a dead world; no-one could be hurt or even mildly upset now by this scrutiny; yet still she felt that they had no right to snoop.

"If you have examples of my grandfather's handwriting in your records," said Peter Blythe, "you can check." He was confident, she knew, that everything would match up. He was insistent that they should check, and his insistence was terribly convincing. "And there are other things in my luggage," he said.

"Luggage?"

"I left it at the station. I came straight here with these few things, so that you would understand it was right for us to talk."

Nell had to concede that he was being meticulous and polite. This Peter, or Pietro, if he were telling the truth, would be justified in being far more antagonistic towards the Johnsons if he felt so inclined. A Johnson had done him out of his inheritance and allowed his grandmother to live under a cloud for the rest of her life.

Nell said: "What really happened to your grandmother, then? I mean, afterwards — after she'd disappeared. Everyone thought — at least, we've learnt

76

recently that most people thought — she'd gone to join her husband."

"But now we know she couldn't have done," said Arthur.

Peter nodded sardonic agreement.

"She went home, then?" said Nell. "To Italy?"

"To Sicily," he said. "Where else could she go?"

The doorknob rattled and turned. Brigid stood in the doorway.

"You said I was to come in . . . ?"

Arthur introduced her with a firmness that told Nell his mind was already made up. He accepted the story and the young man's identity.

"Brigid, this is Peter Blythe. He's Walter Blythe's grandson."

When they sat down again, Peter Blythe edged his chair round so that he could see Brigid. His heavy eyes were sleepily appreciative. While Arthur swiftly sketched in for Brigid's benefit what they had learnt so far, the young man unashamedly studied Brigid's face, her legs, and the line of her forearm along the padded arm of her chair.

When Arthur had filled in the

background, Peter took up the story. He addressed it to Nell and Arthur, but Nell knew from a slight change of timbre in his voice that he was conscious of Brigid all the time. He was set on impressing her with his clarity, his sadness, and his family loyalty. He pulled out all the stops. For the first time Nell was uncritically and unwaveringly glad that Brigid was engaged to Martin Hemming and was so soon going to marry him.

Serafina had lived 'outside Palermo'. That was how Peter phrased it, as though there was no point in going into detail about towns or villages which would mean nothing to people in an English coast resort. It was here that the footloose Walter Blythe had met her, from here that he had impetuously brought her to Lurgate as his wife, and to here that she returned under the cloud of his supposed crime.

Not that she spoke of his crime and his desertion. In a tight, proud Sicilian community the shame of it would have been too much for her. It would have been regarded as a judgment on her for having married an Englishman and left her island.

It was understood that she was a widow. Her husband had died and she had come home. There was nobody to deny it. In those days gossip and scandal did not spread over the world in a matter of hours. Not even in a matter of days or weeks. The ripples did not get far from home. Foreign newspapers weren't flown in on fast planes. The heart of Sicily was as far from Lurgate as it was from the moon.

Serafina Blythe was a respectable widow. That was her story. There was no reason why it should be disbelieved.

"Family honour is a great thing in our land," said Peter Blythe. "Before the first world war it was an almost religious concept. Men and women killed for honour. So it has been with us through the centuries. Family pride was everything. Vendetta was a noble cause. Loss of face, a slight to the family or any member of it, and . . . " he wiped his forefinger significantly across his throat.

"You mean that if any of the family

had known the truth, they'd have tried to avenge her?"

"How could they? To find Walter Blythe and kill him, yes . . . but how? Where? We know now that he was dead anyway, but my grandmother did not know that. So nothing could have been done. They would simply have despised her because her man had left her."

"Wouldn't it have been better for her to have stayed in Lurgate?" asked Brigid. She did not blink under the intense, bold gaze he turned upon her. "If her pride meant so much to her, shouldn't she have faced them out? By disappearing herself, she made it look as though she knew all about the embezzlement and was off to join her husband."

"She did wait ten days or so," her father reminded her. "Perhaps she couldn't understand, and she was waiting to hear from him. And there was no word. Better her home, where the story would be unknown and she could pretend to be a widow, than here, where everybody knew."

Peter nodded as though thanking Arthur for making this easy for him.

Then he resumed his story.

Serafina Blythe had proudly spurned offers of help from Victor Johnson. After what Walter Blythe had done, she hated him and hated all the English. She went back to Sicily and her pride went with her.

She had been home only a week when she realised that she was going to have a child.

Nell tried to think herself into the mind of that flashing, beautiful Italian woman — girl, rather, for she couldn't have been more than twenty-five or so — but the distance was too great. In that day and age, in that primitive community, would one have been able to carry it off with a flourish? She must have had a difficult role thrust on her — having to keep up a pretence of joy that, although her husband was dead, a child was on its way to keep his memory alive. Could she have loved the child, or was it only pride that made it possible for her to keep up the pretence? Did the child, Luigi, remind her too bitterly of the treacherous Walter Blythe, or was she able to love him for himself and be thankful that at least some good had come out of that misery?

Luigi certainly brought further misery to her. He married an English girl, a holidaymaker on the island, a year before the second world war broke out. Serafina and the girl didn't get on.

Peter was born in 1943, and Serafina insisted on referring to him always as Pietro. His father was killed when he was seven.

"Killed?" asked Arthur. "But the war must have been over — I mean, it *was* over. Long before."

"He was among those who welcomed the Allies to Sicily," said Peter. "In 1943 — the year I was born. In Sicily we always had ideas of our own, you understand? We never loved Mussolini. Tyrants from the mainland were never welcome among us. The Mafia made things easy for the Allies, and when peace came the important men of the Mafia were in very good positions. That is how it always is in Sicily." he tried to smile ruefully, to imply with a shrug that he was a civilised young man of the twentieth century who had no time for such things; but there was a spark of arrogant approval which he could not disguise. "But afterwards, many *mafiosi* who had been living in America decided to come back. Their old friends were prospering — why should they not all be friends together? There were many feuds. Many old enmities were revived. My father mixed with the wrong people. One day he went on business to Enna and he was stabbed. Nobody asked why, because nobody would have answered. He was on the wrong side — the side that lost."

"There wasn't anything you could do about it?" It came from Brigid with the force of a challenge.

It was the first time Nell had seen the young man disconcerted. He flushed slowly and sat very still for a moment. Then he forced a rueful smile again. He spread his hands.

"I was seven. You think when I grew up I should practise the vendetta? To seek out and kill my father's killers — and then be killed by one of their family?"

"No, of course not. But . . . "

"When I was old enough to do that, I had other things to do. In Palermo and then in Rome."

He hurried on as though to give her no further chance of questioning him on this embarrassing point.

His mother had married again. Her husband this time was an Italian-American who had returned to Sicily but decided that the States were better after all. Serafina would not meet him. In the world she knew, a widow would never have contemplated marrying again.

"My grandmother," said Peter with a little bow of the head, "held me with her. My mother went to the States with her new man, and I think she was glad to go. I stayed."

In spite of his grandmother's hatred of them, Peter was drawn to the English. He had learnt English from his mother and there was English blood in him from his grandfather and from his mother. "I *think* in English," he said, glancing from Nell to Arthur and then lingeringly to Brigid, perhaps awaiting a nod of recognition or some implicit applause.

But he could not afford to come to England. They were too poor. "And if my grandmother had had the money, I think she would not have given me any of it — not to come to this country." He went eventually to Palermo but his grandmother insisted that he came home regularly. Because of the sacrifices she had made for him, he could not refuse. Not until she died could he go to Palermo for good — and then he was restless and soon on his way to Rome. Again he was a tourist guide.

"I am in Rome a year," he concluded, "when I read in *Il Giorno* a little piece about my grandfather. He is not in South America. He has been in England all the time! So I come." Slowly he appraised the room. "Always I tell myself I will come to England someday. But I did not expect it to be in such circumstances."

They were silent for what seemed an eternity to Nell. There must be a hundred questions still to be asked, but Arthur was exhausted. She wanted to send the young man away. She wanted him out of the house: his eyes were pricing everything, he gave the impression of fingering their possessions and debating whether or not to lay claim to them.

Abruptly Nell said: "Your story's

amazingly circumstantial. Did your grandmother tell you the lot?"

"We were very close."

"But if she was so anxious to keep it
a secret . . . "

"We were very close," he repeated. "I
was all she had. There was no-one else
she could talk to."

Arthur frowned a warning to Nell. He
accepted the story and saw no point in
niggling away at the why and wherefore
of its assembly. She realised that he was
right, but perversely she would have liked
to trip Peter up somehow, somewhere.

Arthur put his elbows on the desk.
Tiredly he said: "What do you want
from me, then?"

"Oh, I have not thought . . . I have not
had time to consider . . . "

"You must have some idea." Tired he
might be, but Arthur could still say
what he meant to say, brushing aside
quibbles and reservations. "A share in
the firm — or a cash payment? Which
have you come for?"

Peter Blythe did not smile too eagerly,
or sigh, or give any sign that he knew
he had pulled it off. There was no hint

of jubilation when he said:

"I thought we would discuss it. Let us get to know one another, yes? I am not here to demand anything, you understand. But I remember my grandmother and what she suffered. Suffered . . . not because of her husband, we now discover, but because of the man who murdered her husband. The murderer . . . "

He left it suggestively in the air.

Nell said: "Have you anywhere to stay in Lurgate?"

"I came straight to you from the station." He got up slowly. Everything about him now was sleek and leisurely. "I must go and find a hotel before it is too late. I do not have much money with me . . . "

"We'll fix it," said Arthur.

"It is kind of you."

"If there's any difficulty, we might fit you in here, but . . . "

"No!" said Peter Blythe quickly. "No, of course you will not wish to do that. You will want to check my story. You will need time. And if I were in your house, at your table, you would not feel free to talk." He picked up his brief-case and

87

put the papers and photographs back into it. He was standing close to Brigid and looking sideways at her — touching her without touching, thought Nell, just as he had done with the room and everything in it. "You will have a great deal to talk about," he said. "And then I think we arrange another meeting."

5

WITH Easter almost upon them, hotel bookings were difficult. Two days, yes. Beyond that, not so easy. And who could say how long Peter Blythe would be staying?

Brigid was glad of the opportunity to ring Martin at Fernrock Hotel and ask him to help them. Perhaps his mother could help a friend of theirs who had just arrived from abroad.

"No need to go into detail," said Arthur. "Just ask if she can rally round."

Nell drove the young man to the station to pick up his luggage.

Arthur had offered to do it but she had overruled him. She was used to taking on the odd jobs. Arthur was so engrossed in business that he tended to leave small duties and routine matters to her. He relied on her. This reliance had frightened her when they were first married. She was a diffident girl, scared of responsibility. Yet because he thought of her as a clear-headed, efficient person she found that she had become one. For years she had felt inadequate with other people but grew brisk and practical because that was how Arthur saw her and how, in time, the others saw her.

By being alone with Peter Blythe while she drove him to the station and the hotel she hoped to discover something about him which had escaped Arthur. She could not have defined exactly what she was expecting: a viciousness that would enable her to hate him, a mistake that would prove he was a fraud, a glimpse of the real person rather than Walter Blythe's self-styled grandson?

But in the car his manner was the same as it had been all evening. He became neither boastful nor more intimate. He was deferential but took it for granted that they were in complete accord and that she recognised the validity of his case.

"I think," he said as they circled the perimeter of the park and headed across town towards the station, "no publicity. Not yet. You agree?"

She could not have agreed more. It

was strange, though, that the suggestion should have come from him. She would have expected him to long for the chance to tell the world of his grandmother's wrongs, of all that she had suffered, and of his own moral inheritance.

"I do not wish to embarrass you," he went on, watching the road ahead with the same possessive curiosity he had shown all evening. "We make our own decisions before the reporters tell stories, yes?"

"I think it would be better," she had to say.

"This hotel you are taking me to . . . ?"

"Utterly reliable," said Nell. "The proprietor is a friend of ours. Brigid — our daughter — is marrying her son a couple of weeks from now."

"Ah." It was a strange, long sigh. She wanted to glance at his profile but did not want him to guess that he had disturbed her. She accelerated, and they raced down the slope towards the railway cutting. "She is a very beautiful girl, your daughter."

"She's a nice girl," said Nell lamely.

"I hope the man is worthy of her."

"Yes," said Nell, very firm now: "he is."

The main road dipped more steeply, and then she had swung into the station approach and they climbed a few yards to the façade of brown brick and green noticeboards. Peter Blythe got out and went to the door that served the enquiry office, goods yard and left luggage office. It was closed. He went into the station through the waiting room. Knowing the vagaries of Lurgate station, Nell thought she ought to get out and help him to track down one of the elusive old men who would be on duty at this time of night. Instead, she stayed where she was. The red light of a signal glowed stolidly above the edge of a roof. A coloured poster faded into monochrome under the station entrance telling her that Harwich was the gate to the Continent. She leaned a few inches out of her window and tried to believe that she could hear the sea. The sound of it against the cliffs and on the beds of pebbles beneath the pier had grown so familiar that it required an effort of will to hear it, from a distance or close at hand.

Peter Blythe came out of the station with two large cases. They were shabby but substantial. It looked as though he had travelled here with every intention of staying.

When the cases had been stowed in the boot and they were driving away, Peter said:

"Your daughter — Brigid, her name?"

Brigid would be sitting with her father at this moment. Nell could so easily visualise them. Brigid would have poured a brandy for Arthur and they would be talking, or sitting meditatively if that was what Arthur wanted. The two of them had always been remarkably in harmony. As a family, thought Nell, we haven't done badly; not at all badly.

Now who was wallowing in her family pride? The Sicilians weren't the only ones.

"Yes," she said. "That's right. Brigid."

"She will talk to this man. If she is marrying him so soon, she will tell him everything."

"Probably." Nell hadn't thought of that, but could not deny that he was right. "But it'll stay in the family. Mrs Hemming won't chatter to people outside."

"You are sure?"

"Does it matter?"

"No. No, it does not matter. But you and I, we can talk better if not everybody else is talking at the same time, I think."

"We'll tell Mrs Hemming only as much as she needs to know," Nell assured him. "And you'll be quieter there, in the hotel with a lot of others, than you would be if you stayed with us." She slowed for traffic lights. "Sooner or later there's bound to be some publicity, whether you stay or go."

She admitted to herself that she was probing, hoping for him to indicate what his plans were. He did not reply, but peered up at a new block of shops and flats going up on the intersection.

He said: "Are Blythe and Johnson . . . I mean, is Mr Johnson building these?"

"It's a development by a builder from Maidstone."

"Ah — competition?"

"We don't run the entire town, you know."

"You need a Mafia." Peter laughed more loudly than seemed justifiable.

"Does it really still . . . "

Nell stopped herself. It would sound too patronising to ask if such barbaric societies still held their old sway in modern times. She was sure she had read something about it somewhere but was left with only the memory of improbable melodrama. To ask questions would imply that she believed lurid newspapers and lurid films.

But if she was shirking, he wasn't. He was quick to pick her up. As the lights changed and she sped away up the winding road to the hotel, he said:

"You think time can change the timeless? The Mafia is still there. Not as strong as in the old days — you can escape from it now, you can take a bus into Palermo and fly in an aeroplane to the mainland and cease to be a Sicilian — but it is still alive. No more bandits and farm bosses: now it is a big power in property development. All new and modern, but still the same. You understand? Perhaps it is in my blood, too. Perhaps I can help you here in Lurgate!" Again he laughed.

Taking it for granted, she thought dismally, that he's going to be brought into the firm and looked after. No demands, he had said. But here was the hint of one of the demands he would sooner or later make.

They reached Fernrock Hotel. The porter shuffled out from behind the desk and, after strenuously denying that there was a room to spare, accepted her word that the arrangement had been made by phone with Mrs Hemming. He groaned over the cases and tottered towards the lift with them, followed by Peter Blythe.

Just as the lift was scraping up to the second floor, Mrs Hemming came along the corridor from the dining room.

"Oh, it's you, Mrs Johnson. You've brought your friend?"

"He's just gone upstairs. He'll be down to sign the register in a few minutes, I expect."

"I've just made myself some coffee," said Mrs Hemming. It was her equivalent of an invitation.

They went through into her sitting room. Nell wondered how much to say; whether, indeed, to say anything. But Brigid would talk to Martin and Martin would talk to his mother, and it was better that she should not be taken by surprise and have reason to be surly about it afterwards.

Nell said: "Betty . . . "

It was difficult to get the name out. Several times before she had tried to get them on to Christian name terms, without success. Obstinately, in spite of the impending marriage of their children, they remained Mrs Hemming and Mrs Johnson.

"Taken by surprise, were you?" said Mrs Hemming. She reached for the coffee pot. "Black or white? I like it black."

"Black, thank you."

"Hm."

"Yes, we weren't expecting this . . . this friend."

"From abroad, Martin said. Or that's what Brigid led him to think. Foreign?"

"Half foreign," said Nell. "English extraction." She took a deep breath. "I hope you won't say anything to anyone, but . . . "

"Who says I gossip about my guests?"

"Nobody. Of course not. That's why we particularly wanted him to come here."

"Something funny about him?"

"His name's Peter Blythe," said Nell.

"Hm. Doesn't sound very foreign to me." Then Mrs Hemming's fingers tightened on the sugar bowl as she was about to push it towards Nell. Her knuckles were white and skeletal. "Blythe?" she said. "Blythe? You mean . . . some relation's turned up?"

"Walter's grandson."

There was a faint rustle of plumbing within the wall. Somewhere a door slammed. There was a gust of radio music, turned up and hurriedly turned down.

Mrs Hemming said: "No."

"I promise you it came as a great surprise to us, but . . . "

"No." It was almost a shout. "It's rubbish. He never had a son, let alone a grandson. Or a daughter. Or . . . "

"A son," said Nell. "Apparently she didn't know until after the disappearance. After she herself had gone away."

She reached for the cup of coffee which Mrs. Hemming had poured for her, but Mrs Hemming's arm was rigidly in the way, her hand still clamped on the sugar bowl. It did not move. She said vehemently:

"And you've listened to a tale like that? You're letting someone put that over on you?"

"The evidence . . . "

"Evidence? How could there be any evidence for a pack of lies? I never heard of anything like it. Never in all my born days."

Nell was speechless. She could have expected a show of surprise, but this outburst baffled her. Mrs Hemming was pale with rage. She could not have been more indignant if Nell had come here to say that they had decided her precious Martin wasn't good enough for Brigid and that the wedding was to be considered off.

Martin . . . that must be it. She was afraid of the consequences to him. She wanted the Johnson firm and the Johnson money for her son: she didn't want it shared with a descendant of Walter Blythe.

It was a grubby, distasteful thought. Nell tried to push it aside. She tried again: "Betty, you mustn't imagine for one moment . . . "

"I'd like to see this impostor."

"Please. We've asked you to find accommodation for him because we trust you. We don't want gossip or publicity until we've sorted everything out. If you're going to take against him for some reason . . . "

"For some reason!" Mrs Hemming echoed despairingly.

Then she sat back, breathing hard. Outside there was the faint tinkle of the bell from the reception desk and the sound of shuffling footsteps. It was followed by the clank of the lift gate being closed.

Mrs Hemming got up. She went to the door and opened it. Nell stood up, but did not dare to go too close.

Over Mrs Hemming's shoulder she saw Peter Blythe crossing the hall from the lift to the desk. Then he was obscured from her view as Mrs Hemming walked out to meet him.

Nell forced herself to turn towards her cup of coffee. She drank it, and poured herself another cup. At the end of five minutes Mrs Hemming returned and closed the door behind her.

"Peter Blythe," she said accusingly.

"The name doesn't really fit, does it?" Nell ventured. "He does look so Italian." She hesitated, then asked: "Would you sooner we tried somewhere else?"

"He can stay."

Nell drove home slowly. She felt weak. She was battered and bewildered. She had to force herself to concentrate on the road and drive steadily. With luck she would be able to get home. There would come a moment when she would simply have to throw up her hands and cry enough, that's enough, no more. She wanted someone to take over control of the car, to put it away in the garage, to lift her out and to put her to bed.

When she walked slowly and delicately into the house as though treading on some brittle treasure, she found that Brigid had gone up to her room. Arthur was waiting, his eyes lined with dark rims.

"All set?" he said. "All tucked up and comfy?"

"I wish *I* were."

"Darling — do you feel as grim as I do?"

She went slowly up to him and put her head against his shoulder. His chin dabbed her hair. He nudged her face up towards his and kissed her.

He said: "You've got beautiful ears. But I've told you that before, haven't I?"

"I don't mind being told again."

Because he had said this about her ears years ago and because so obviously meant what he said — Nell had kept her hair short and severe so that her ears were always visible. She relaxed. He steered her towards the stairs. Vaguely she felt that this was all wrong: he was the one who was tired, the one with the heaviest responsibility to bear, the one who had to face all the unpalatable decisions; she ought to be looking after him, making things easy for him. But it was a relief to have him taking charge of her. She let him push her gently, tenderly towards their bedroom.

"I'll run your bath," he said.

"No." The effort of getting into the bath and drying herself afterwards was too great. Just the thought of the effort was too great. "Not tonight. I just want to collapse."

"Leave some space for me. I'm pretty collapsible myself right now."

When they were in bed and the lights were out, she told him about Mrs Hemming's reactions. "You must have imagined it," he said. She tried to argue with him, and he said: "We're all a bit keyed-up. Frankly, I can't see straight, and I don't suppose you can either." She wanted to persist, but her tongue grew slurred and drowsy.

It might have been a few minutes later or a few hours — but no, he would hardly have woken her up in the middle of the night just to mumble about Brigid — when she was sure he said: "Rivalry . . . handsome young Latin type on the scene . . . Martin'll have to hold on like grim death. Still, he's coming into the straight. He ought to be all right." Nell tried to tell him that Peter Blythe wasn't Brigid's type, but not so long ago she had been saying that Martin wasn't Brigid's type, and now she hated the thought of Martin not being strong enough to hold on.

She must have said something without knowing it, for Arthur muttered: "Didn't

103

know you were such a xenophobe."

"I'm not, but I don't want ... don't want ... "

She hadn't the energy to finish the sentence. Maybe it was all a dream anyway. All she was sure of was that she didn't want Peter Blythe under her roof and didn't want him near her husband or daughter.

6

THE gulls flew in from the sea and along the estuary like enemy aircraft and swooped greedily on to the ridges of a ploughed field. The sun was bright and the cars from London were already creeping in on Lurgate. It was literally a matter of creeping: somewhere along the main coast road there was a traffic jam, and metal and tempers grew hot as time went by and only a trickle of cars squeezed through.

Brigid drove inland along the main road for a mile, then branched off and headed for the low foot-hills.

Peter said: "You must not frown when you drive."

"The sun's in my eyes."

"It is not that. You are too serious. If you frown, you will get lines round your eyes. And you are too beautiful for that."

Brigid continued to look at the road and at the same time tried to let the muscles of her face relax without allowing him to see that she was obeying him.

He said: "You would like me to drive? Then you may look at the scenery."

"I know the scenery," she said. "You don't. The idea is for me to drive while you look at it."

"You are kind. I am not used to it, you understand. Always I show people round and point out this mountain and that bay. I do the running commentary. But here I know nothing."

She was not sure whether this meant that he would like her to point out the main landmarks. Trying to think of something interesting to say, she realised how little she knew about the most familiar scenes all around her. They were running parallel with the coast for a short distance, and she could have pointed out the curve of the bay . . . and then added what? It was Lurgate Bay, and that was that. The Vikings had been here in the past, but she didn't know how often or what they had done — nothing they hadn't done everywhere else, she supposed. The electricity pylons marched across the levels and stumped into the hills; and they were simply electricity pylons.

Brigid said: "There are some interesting old churches further inland. But I don't know if you're particularly keen . . . "

"I am at your mercy."

Seawards, a row of red and white chalets perched on the sea wall as though on an assembly line. Below them was a caravan site, a town on wheels, ready to run for it if the sea broke through the wall.

"You are doing it again," said Peter.

"Mm?"

"You are making the faces. You must not frown. Do not take life too seriously. Do not be too English."

"You're half English," said Brigid. And because of this sensation of his needling her, she needled back. "At least, that's your story."

"Half English," he acknowledged. "But not all. I am not so serious. I am not bitter."

"Nor am I."

"Let your hair down," he said.

His fluent English twisted down odd by-ways from time to time. Some of his slang phrases were up to date, some had an archiac ring. North Country expressions mingled with fragments of Knightsbridge patter, only to be shaken up and rattled against a fistful of Americanisms. One could play quite a fascinating game working out the origins of the people he had shown round Palermo and Rome — the things he had learnt from them while they supposed themselves to be learning from him.

"We may stop here?" he said.

Obediently she drew in on the grass verge. They had reached the first ridge, a shallow petrified wave breaking on the edge of the coastal plain. Beyond were the orchards, their blossom foaming in the troughs of the rolling landscape.

"It must look strange to you," she ventured. "Very different from what you're used to."

"Yes. It is so green. So much green — the land and the sea. In my country it is harder. All much harder and brighter. In my country" — his lips drew back from his teeth — "we are more . . . more certain. Your green, it has not made up its mind. But our rocks and trees and

108

the sea — the red and the brown and the blue, all so very definite. You must come one day and see them."

"We're going to Malta after the wedding," said Brigid.

"Ah. Malta." He shrugged. "So."

He had been looking out across the land but now he focused disconcertingly on her. His eyes gloated; they were repellent and impersonal. Yet she wasn't prudish and she wasn't a hypocrite, and she had to admit that his sheer animal vitality plucked a chord within her.

She shifted in her seat and pointed over the orchards to the long white concrete boxes of the research centre, two miles away.

"That's where Martin works."

"So. Your Martin. He is what — a fruit packer?"

"Certainly not."

Peter laughed. He put his hand on her knee. When she jerked away, he smiled as though it did not matter in the least. He had all the time in the world.

"It is no bad thing," he said, "a packer of fruit. But go on. You will tell me, what does he do?"

She had no wish to tell him. She would have preferred him to talk about himself. Although her mother and father had asked her nothing specific when they knew Peter had been urging her to spend an afternoon showing him the countryside, she knew that they looked forward to her returning with some indication of what his plans were, how he envisaged the pay-off, just what was in his mind. Tonight he was to have a final vetting by old Mr Farnham. If there was anything they should know before then, it would be a good thing for Brigid to learn about it.

But Peter was playing the part of a leisurely young tourist, not merely allowing her to do the talking but expecting her to do it.

"Martin," she said reluctantly, "works on pest control."

She was sure he would grin, and he did — pretending to conceal it but not really meaning to keep it too secret.

"That must be important," he said. "The world needs to control pests."

"He spent two years at the agricultural college" — she waved vaguely beyond the further, higher shadows of the

110

downs — "and then they took him on at the laboratories here. It's a centre for studying the effects of chemical insecticides — not just the direct properties, but possible side-effects."

"Worthy," Peter nodded. "Very worthy."

She had told him the basic facts and had no intention of telling him any more. She would not expose her love and enthusiasm to his cynical examination. To her, Martin was like one of the atom scientists with an acutely sensitive conscience about the possible use or misuse of his work: like those physicists who had struggled to limit the applications of atomic power, he was both a scientist and a watchdog. He believed in careful experiment and rigid control. He was painstaking in checking for side-effects and for long-term dangers. If he felt it was too soon for an untried poison to be put on the market, he was capable of working against his own employers. Recent deaths of birds and animals, and the indications of possible illness in human beings, had persuaded them that even in stubborn opposition he was valuable to them.

Peter Blythe was not the kind of man

who would understand all this. These were not his values. He would deride them; make them sound stodgy and unadventurous.

And what was so superior about *him*? A tourist guide, probably cunning and unscrupulous, knowing all the rackets. A young man who had come to Lurgate in search of an easy living.

There was no reason why her father should not simply send him away.

But she knew he wouldn't.

"And you?" he said.

"Me?"

"Your job," he said. "Or perhaps you have never needed to work. Of course. With Johnson's to look after you, and now a distinguished husband to take you over . . . "

"I worked in London," she said hotly, "for a scientific publisher. And it was hard work. At the moment I'm free-lancing — some technical sub-editing, and some indexing. And when we're married I'm not just going to twiddle my thumbs while Martin works; we couldn't afford it. I'll carry on with the editorial side."

"Ah, yes. And you will be able to help your husband."

"I can certainly look after this records . . ."

"And one day he will write a big treatise on all those bugs of his. His life's work."

"How do you know?"

"They do," said Peter. "These serious people — so admirable — they all do. They're all bitten by the bug." He let out a surprisingly high-pitched giggle.

"You make it sound silly," said Brigid. "And dull. And it's not."

"He is fortunate, your Martin," said Peter. His voice dropped to a seductive murmur. "Very fortunate."

Brigid slammed the car into gear and jolted off the verge on to the road. She drove inland, letting him make what he chose of the villages and orchards they passed. They had gone for more than five minutes in silence when he let out an exclamation.

Brigid slowed. "What is it?"

"This building — please, we look?"

They were approaching a large country pub. The inn sign stood in a small circular lawn surrounded by flowerbeds, and beyond a low red brick wall there was a garden with metal tables and chairs. It was The Dumb Woman. The picture on the inn sign, recently repainted, showed a fat woman huddled on the ground with two burly farmers sitting on her head trying to fit a muzzle over her face.

"So this is The Dumb Woman," said Peter.

"You've heard of it?"

"It has been here a long time, I think."

"Two or three hundred years." Even this she couldn't be sure of. She just knew that the old pub was referred to as being 'historic'. "It's been done up recently," she said, "but I don't think they've spoilt it." She waited a moment, then asked again: "You've heard of it?"

"My grandmother mentioned it. I asked her once about England and how it was like home. Or not like home. I was always asking her about England. And she told me that my grandfather — this was a long time ago, before she told me the truth about him deserting her and that it was not true how she told us she was a widow . . . only of course now we know it *was* true, but . . . "

"All right," said Brigid. "All right. We've gone all over that. It makes my head whirl. Go on."

"Yes. Like I tell you, I ask all the time about England. I ask if the hostaria are like ours. And if the men stand outside in the street talking all the time — in my town, you know, they go in for a quick drink and then come out and lean against a wall in the piazza and talk. But my grandmother tell me that in England the men shut themselves inside these places and talk. They do not like to talk in the open. And she says that The Dumb Woman is a big place outside Lurgate where my grandfather comes. Especially when he has his big motor-car. I remember . . . I hear her voice now." He put his head back and half-closed his eyes. "I ask her what it is like inside, and she says — I hear her say it — 'He would not take a *lady* there'. Not a lady," he mused. Then his eyes opened again and somehow became deeper and darker. He chuckled. "May I take *you* inside? I think it is a different world now. In England they are not so strict any more."

"But in England," said Brigid, "they're still strict about the licensing laws. It doesn't open till six o'clock."

"So. Twenty minutes only."

"We ought to be turning back," said Brigid.

She thought he was about to argue. Instead, he put his hand on her arm and let it slide a few inches towards her wrist.

"May I drive on the way back?"

"Well . . . I don't know that Mummy . . . "

"Your mother's car will be safely brought home to Lurgate. You ain't never seen driving like mine, baby."

She could not tell whether this was a send-up or whether the words came merely as an echo of something once picked up which he now thought would be appropriate.

She said: "If you'll promise to be careful . . . "

"You think because I work in Rome I am a mad driver? All Italians are mad drivers?"

He got out of the car and walked

round to her side. Brigid opened her door and slid across into the seat he had just been occupying. Peter stooped and got in. As he leaned over the wheel, his head darted suddenly forward and he kissed her. Brigid jolted backwards. His hand reached for her shoulder.

"No," she said.

"Such a wonderful day," he said. "And you, and the sunshine. The atmosphere — you do not feel it? You are not intoxicated by it?"

"No."

"Ah." He let himself slide back and face the wheel. He pulled his door shut. "But you must not blame me if I am carried away."

"You weren't carried away," she said. "You're a tryer-on. It's just a reflex with you."

He started the car and they moved smoothly away. "Like all Italian men," he, sighed. "They drive like maniacs, and they have reflex actions when they see beautiful women. You do not take me seriously, no?"

"So soon?"

"Ah." He pounced. "It is just a matter

117

of time, then? It is only my timing is wrong?"

"No," said Brigid. "It's all wrong. You know the route? Turn left at the end here."

He was a fast driver and a good one. Either he had a good sense of direction or, in spite of his apparent indifference, he had efficiently memorised the route on their journey out here: she did not need to dictate the turnings to him, but could feel him starting to slow just at the moment when she herself would have slowed for a particular corner. His right hand rested lightly on the wheel but was alive and alert, ready to act in a split second.

Airily he said: "You will inherit a lot of money, I think?"

"I don't see what it's . . . "

"In the old days," he went on without turning his head, "they favoured the amalgamation of families at a time like this. A good idea, don't you think? A swell idea. Unions of princes and princesses of industry, just as there were unions of royal families. They favoured alliance rather than war."

"Meaning you expect to be at war with me sooner or later?" said Brigid uneasily.

"I hope not. I do not see any reason why we should be at war. Now, let us be serious for a minute. Just one minute. You know I do not like always to be too serious. But if we are sensible about an alliance . . . "

"I don't know what kind of alliance you mean," said Brigid. "And I'd remind you I'm getting married."

"Of course. For you it is not the prince and princess story. It is the one about the peasant boy who wins the hand of the princess. But that is not the only possible happy ending, I think. When the rightful prince comes back from exile to claim his own, I think the peasant boy makes a noble farewell and walks off into the sunset."

"I thought you were telling fairy tales," said Brigid. "Now we seem to be mixed up in a bad film."

"To me it is still a fairy tale. Jack the Insect-Killer."

They were racing across the levels towards Lurgate. The sea wall ended in the steep incline of the cliff. The town hall tower, a spindly little belfry, shone against the sky. But not, thought Brigid, in any way like a fairy castle. She said: "I don't see what you're trying to do. Martin and I are going to be married. I love him."

"The situation has changed."

"It hasn't changed. Not so far as I am concerned. All through this mess and gossip of the last couple of weeks Martin's been just the same as ever. He's loyal . . . "

"Why should he not be loyal? The money's still good. Though it'll be interesting," said Peter, "to see how he reacts when he finds there may not be quite as much for him as he expected."

"He didn't expect anything," said Brigid. "He's not marrying me for money."

"It is so magnificent, how you spring to his defence."

They reached the outskirts of the town. Brigid made him stop so that she could take the wheel once more. "Just in case."

"You think I look too masterful, in charge of your mother's car? It could be bad taste, taking charge so soon. I know the English worry always about the taste being bad." Peter got out and paced round the car with an exaggeratedly stately tread. When he had moved in beside her and slammed the door he said: "I shall buy myself a big car. Very big, very fast. Bright red. When I can afford it." He flashed her a smile. "When do you think that will be?"

"I've no idea."

She drove him to the hotel. He had time to wash and change before coming to dinner with them.

"And I bring my testimonials for your Mr Farnham."

When he got out of the car he bent as though to kiss her hand. Instead, he kissed the inside of her wrist and straightened up very slowly.

Brigid drove home.

She had a quick bath and put on a loose summer dress splashed with turquoise flowers. By the time she came downstairs, Mr Farnham had arrived. The door of the study was open and she could hear the intermittent, wobbly crackle of his voice as her father poured him a drink and they talked politely while they waited. The formalities were a strain. Her father wanted to get to grips with Peter Blythe and have everything settled, cut and dried; and Mr Farnham was dithering with impatient curiosity.

Her mother crossed the hall. Their paths converged. Nell was almost too elegant. She had encased herself in an armour of smartness. Everything about her was too tight, too tense, too aggressive.

"Cheer up, Mummy."

Brigid kissed her.

The front door bell rang. Nell opened it, and Peter came in with his brief-case, bulging this time. They shook hands and made conventional noises. Peter looked Brigid up and down and said: "Charming. Oh, so charming."

Nell offered to take the brief-case from him but he shook his head politely and tightened his grip on it, making it clear that he preferred to keep it with him.

Nell said: "I hope the hotel's comfortable?"

"Comfortable, yes."

"Mrs Hemming keeps up a very high standard."

"Yes. I have only one complaint."

"Oh?"

"My luggage has been searched. My luggage and the drawers where I put things."

Brigid and Nell stared incredulously.

"You do not believe me?" he said. "But I promise you it is so. Someone in the hotel has searched my cases — turned over everything. It is put back most carefully, but I know; I can tell."

"I'm sure you must have made a mistake," said Nell frigidly. "If you've mislaid something . . . "

"No, no. Nothing is missing." Peter tapped his brief-case. "I have it all with me."

"Then what would be the point of going through your things? Who'd have done such a thing?"

"That is what I ask myself."

Peter looked ironically, quizzically at Brigid.

7

NEXT day the reporters were back and the telephone was ringing with renewed fervour.

"It was bound to happen," said Brigid's father. "I suppose Amy couldn't keep her mouth shut. She must have had a pretty good idea of what's been going on, and she's been showing off to her friends."

"Or that old fool Farnham," said her mother. "He'll have been doddering round telling all his cronies this morning."

Nell did not try to hide her antagonism towards Mr Farnham. Brigid had watched it emerging at dinner the previous evening. Mr Farnham could not really be reproached: he had been objective and thorough, covering all the ground they had wanted him to cover; but the fact that he had robbed her of any lingering hope she might have had of the whole business collapsing had turned her mother against him.

Mr Farnham had been enthralled. He

recognised the travelling clock — he and his late wife had seen it several times when visiting the Blythes — and there was no doubt about the identity of the young woman in the photographs. That was Serafina: no doubt about it. He questioned Peter at length, and the answers rang true. Mr Farnham made it clear that his own testimony ought to be sufficient for anyone. But if further proof were required, why not approach the police — or, if it was out of their province, at least telephone Rome and Palermo for confirmation. Peter laughed and agreed. It would take time — the carabiniere were suspicious of outsiders, the local police tended to be uncommunicative — "And it's hardly a matter on which we can call on Interpol," Arthur observed. But there were channels that could be used. Brigid sensed that her father was reluctant to push matters to such an extreme. The evidence was already enough for him. It was Peter who urged him to tie up every last thread.

"You speak to Rome. I give you the address of the tourist office and they will tell you who I am. And the Palermo office — they know that I am who I say I am. It is a lot of trouble to speak to my own town — you need an interpreter, I think — but you want to try, you try. They tell you who I am and where I live. And about my grandmother. Please, I wish you to be happy."

Brigid, enmeshed in the growing complexities of the affair, wondered if his insistence was merely a bluff. He might be encouraging them with such apparent frankness simply in order to persuade them that it wasn't really necessary to go any further. He had all the makings of a gambler, of the con man her mother would still prefer him to be. This could be his biggest gamble. Yet would he risk such a bluff being called? The layers of possibility and probability were too confusing: truth overlaid by exaggeration yet nevertheless basically the truth . . . or falsehood covered by plausibility and brightly veneered with additional falsehood?

Mr Farnham at any rate was convinced. In his view, nobody could have made all this up. The picture and documents were authentic. Everything fitted. He even claimed that he would have recognised the boy at once: he had Serafina's face and Walter Blythe's hair.

Peter played up to him as though revelling in the opportunity of showing how well he had mastered his role. He treated it all with the light seriousness of a skilled exponent of the most delicate tragi-comedy.

This, Mr Farnham asserted, was undoubtedly Walter Blythe's grandson.

Brigid agreed with her mother that it was probably old Farnham who blabbed the story all over town as soon as he was up and about this following morning.

The reporters' questions were like a resumed hammering, a head-aching noise that had abated but was now starting up again. Did Mr Johnson have a further statement to make? Was it true that a claimant had arrived and that he showed every sign of being genuine? What was the story behind it . . . could they say that an agreement had been reached . . . an agreement was being reached . . . Mr Johnson stood by his offer to make restitution . . . the name of Blythe would be restored to the firm . . . ?

Peter arrived at the house, dodged a pimply young man from the *Lurgate and Eastweald Gazette* (with which were combined the *Blackstable Advertiser*, the *Surriham Chronicle* and the *Tidway Gazette*) and demanded to see Mr Johnson. Arthur had gone out to give instructions to the foreman on the new housing estate, but had promised to be back within the hour.

Nell and Brigid had coffee with Peter in the sitting room at the back of the house. The door bell and telephone bell rang simultaneously. Amy dealt, with the caller at the door, and they let the telephone ring until it finally gave up.

Peter. said: "We must reach our decisions quickly."

Nell made a slow ritual of opening the biscuit barrel and offering it to him. "I think it's for my husband to decide . . . "

"We want to prevent speculation. They will make such silly stories in the newspapers. Let us settle it so they cannot invent things."

Brigid saw that his mood was toughening. This was not like the lightheartedness of the last few days. The taut wire was straining.

He had said he was not here to demand anything. His approach had been friendly and leisurely. But he had been sizing up the situation and, after Mr Farnham's support last night, had doubtless decided he was in control. He knew his own strength and was now ready to apply the pressure.

Peter caught her eye. She was conscious of his making an effort to slip back into his old casual manner. He looked away, smiling at Nell.

"Maybe I ask for the hand of the princess in marriage as well? That is the accepted thing, is it not?"

Nell put her cup down with a bang. "I think you're too late," was all she could find to say.

"Much too late," Brigid confirmed.

"There was a girl in one of the parties I showed round Rome," said Peter lazily. "A very pretty girl. Not so pretty as Brigid, but pretty. She was on holiday with her mother. When they went home she was going to marry. She tell me all this. People tell me so much, you know.

But there is another young man in the party, and I do not have to watch very carefully to see what is happening. I do not think she married the poor man at home. All the time I see people change . . . ”

There was the faint thud of the front door closing. Brigid's father came in, opening and closing doors, looking for them. When he reached the sitting room, Peter was already standing.

“I think we must talk.”

The two of them went off to the study.

Afterwards, when Peter had gone, there was an awkward silence in which Brigid and her mother waited to hear what had been discussed. For once her father was uncommunicative. Under their enquiring gaze he said at last:

“This is for me to settle. It's my responsibility.”

“What's he up to?” demanded Nell at once. “If he's trying to talk you into something, I want to . . . ”

“He can't make up his mind. He knows he's on to a good thing and I think he's not sure how to play it.”

"Darling, you know there's no legal responsibility in this. We've already been told that. If you want to throw him out and say to hell with the gossip, we'll stand by you. You know that. Even if there's a lawsuit. Even if we lose . . . "

"Yes," he said, "I know. But you'll have to leave it to me."

"Make him wait!" said Nell savagely. "Why is he so afraid of publicity? That's what has triggered him off today. If he's got something to hide, make him wait until it comes out into the open. Check with Rome, check with Palermo . . . and if there *is* something wrong, and there's a chance of his nerve cracking . . . "

"He's Walter Blythe's grandson," said Arthur. "I'm sure of that. So are we all. So even if he's been in prison or is wanted for pinching a tourist's purse or raping someone's daughter, it doesn't affect the main issue. In fact, you could say that if in some ways he's an undesirable character, it's my father's fault. The Johnsons are to blame for depriving him of the advantages he ought to have had. I'm sorry, love — you married into a bad family."

"I won't let you say that."

"It's my responsibility. I've got to try and do what's right." He said again: "You'll have to leave it to me."

Easter weekend was upon them with squalls and sunshine, cars and coaches and crowded trains. A Royal Marine band from Chatham played on the pier. From the promenade one got the impression that the band was striking pinched, tinny little echoes from the shore, but these were in fact the spluttering voices of a hundred transistor radios. At one point between the old town and the promenade the gusts of wind across the bay gave victory first to the smell of fresh fish, then to that of fried fish and chips.

Brigid and Martin spent Friday in their new flat. The carpets had been delivered and the curtains were ready for hanging.

There was a constraint between them which neither would admit. Brigid could not tell him of Peter's accusation that someone in the hotel had for some reason gone through his luggage, yet everything else seemed trivial. She knew it was not true; but until the matter was brought out and settled it was not enough to know that it was not true, because in fact she didn't know it wasn't true. Her head ached.

They manoeuvred the carpets into position. A few weeks ago they had been laughing delightedly at the prospect of these jobs and the eventual result. Now they worked in silence.

Brigid was frightened. Even with the carpets down the place seemed hollow. It was empty, and it would never be filled. Martin had brought two margarine boxes filled with books and he set these out on the shelves built into the alcove where the room turned. But they did not belong.

She and Martin would never live here.

Her stomach turned over.

"It's all going to fall down." She was startled to hear that she had cried it aloud.

Martin patted two books into position. "You're not accusing your father of being a jerry-builder?"

"All of it," she said. "Our life. It's going to come to bits."

He came swiftly away from the book-shelves as though intent on striking her.

He took her by the shoulders and looked into her eyes. His hands were hard and firm but his voice was gentle.

"Brigid . . . darling Brigid . . . what on earth are you talking about?"

"It's not going to work out."

"You're raving, love. You've got to stop."

"I can't help it."

"You can help it." His hands and voice tightened. "What's all this about? If it's something to do with that slimy little rat from Rome, or wherever . . . "

"He's not slimy."

"Isn't he? You like him?"

"I didn't say . . . "

"He's been feeding you with some of his precious ideas, I suppose. He wants everything he can get out of the Johnson family — you included. And you don't find him unattractive? Are you making excuses to yourself because you find him attractive — getting upset because you're wondering how to break it to me, when you haven't even got round to breaking it to yourself yet? Come on, be honest."

"Is that what you think?" she blazed at him.

"What do you expect me to think?"

For the first time, staggeringly, he shook her. She could not twist her shoulders away from him. He held on and shook her violently, possessively to and fro.

"Martin . . . "

"I don't believe it," he said. "I know I'm talking rubbish — but not nearly as much rubbish as you." He wasn't shouting at her. He was just steady and deliberate and utterly determined. "I don't believe this Peter or Pietro can get anywhere near you — but I don't want even a whisper of it. You belong to me."

"Yes," she whispered.

"And you'll stop talking nonsense."

"Yes."

"I know you're upset, and this whole business is a pain in the neck. But it's nothing to do with us. Not really with *us* — you and me. It's not going to stop us getting married and living happily ever after."

Nuts to the prince coming back to claim his own, she thought.

"Martin," she said, "I do love you."

"Good." At last he released her. "And now you can get on with those curtains."

"Yes, sir. Anything you say, sir."

The rest of the day was as it ought to be. If every now and then she felt that it wasn't so simple to dismiss Peter Blythe and that he wasn't as trivial as Martin would like him to be, she suppressed these doubts. And as to Peter's luggage having been searched — no, that was a mistake. He had imagined it.

Saturday dawned bright. The main road was a funnel decanting more and more visitors into Lurgate. It was impossible that the town should hold any more, yet still they poured in. The sensible thing was to stay indoors, but Bank Holiday weekends had a maddening lure — the awful drawing power of a really repulsive horror film.

Brigid and Martin walked along the promenade, jostled against the rail or into the gutter. Lurgate was their home; they could stroll here more comfortably on any other Sunday during the year; but like so many of the local inhabitants they were sucked into the whirlpool of strangers.

As they reached the entrance to the pier, Peter Blythe forced his way through the crowds to join them.

"A friendly face!" he said. "Two friendly faces!"

Martin looked stonily at him.

Peter managed to insinuate himself between them, linking arms with Brigid and putting a conspiratorial hand on Martin's shoulder.

"We English must stick together!"

He was drawing them off the promenade on to the wooden slats of the pier, with the dull yellow of sand and pebbles glinting up through the cracks. Martin came to a halt.

"We don't want to go along there."

"We try our skill, yes?"

"It's not a matter of skill," said Martin. "All the games are loaded against you."

"Then we find a way of shifting the load. Come, I show you. We have the contest."

"Not for me."

"You do not enjoy losing?" said Peter gently.

Brigid found that they were continuing along the pier, until the colour between the planks changed to a flickering bluish-green.

Peter stopped to examine a fruit machine. He put in a penny and lost it. The next time, he won twopence. His progress was as slow as a child's. He wanted to study everything. When they came to a rifle range, Martin said:

"They're badly balanced. You can't work out the compensation."

Peter took a gun and fired three shots at random. Then he nodded. He spent a shilling, and won a plastic teddy-bear which he thrust into Brigid's arms.

Martin grimly took out some money. He lost.

They began to play in ludicrous earnest. They rolled pennies, pulled levers, aimed wooden balls at crockery cats. Peter played with a wealth of flamboyant gestures and sounds. He leaned over pennies and crooned at them in Italian, coaxed them, waved spells. His imprecations when he missed a shot or lost a coin might have been designed to cow the boards and machines into submission next time. He sang out in joy when he won. And it had to be admitted that he won — often.

Martin was dogged and pessimistic. He did not abandon himself as Peter did. It was not that he was surly in defeat: he simply did not have Peter's faith in luck and invocations, and so he lost more often. Brigid felt very fond of him because he was so completely and consistently Martin.

At the same time she felt uneasy when she realised how much her acute awareness of him was due to Peter's presence. When Peter went away — if he went away — perhaps everything would be dulled again; everything would return comfortably to normal.

"No flea circus?" Peter was asking. His head bobbed inquiringly at Martin. "Not so much fun for you if there is no flea circus, I think. Brigid has told me how you love insects."

"Love?" said Martin gruffly. "I don't know about that. They're my job, that's all. I spend my time finding ways of getting rid of them."

"Ah. A love-hate relationship. That is what the trick-cyclists say. We English" — he grimaced with his plump, sensual, very un-English lower lip — "are so strange, don't you think? Animal lovers and animal killers."

They stopped, again prompted by Peter, at a fortunetelling machine. Martin drew the line at this, but Peter put in a penny and cheerfully watched the pointer spinning. A purple-printed card dropped into the tray. He picked it up and read it greedily.

"I will meet a beautiful girl and be fortunate in a financial investment. But the tense is wrong." He bowed to Brigid. "I have already met the beautiful girl."

"Let's hope you're luckier with your financial investment," said Martin.

"There is no reason why I should not have success with both."

"One very good reason," said Martin: "me."

"You, too — you desire both?"

"I'm marrying Brigid. That's all that matters to me. Is that clear?"

"Then why," said Peter with the swiftness of a knife thrust into the ribs, "did you wish to find out about my claim — to learn what evidence I had? You or your mother, or both of you — so interested in my papers."

"I haven't a clue what you're on about."

"My room. You search my room."

"Now, just a minute . . . "

"You go through my papers."

"Are you trying to be funny?"

"I do not think it is funny."

Martin took a step towards him. Brigid gasped and tried to catch his arm but he shook her off. Peter laughed without mirth. Martin grabbed at him and, as he tried to dodge, got a grip on his tie. They lurched against a weighing machine. Its platform rattled.

"Hey, you two . . . "

A pink, plump woman with a moustache stamped along the echoing boarding. Over her shoulder was a leather satchel full of coppers which thumped and jangled against her as she walked.

"Martin," Brigid implored him. "Please. We've had enough publicity as it is."

This seemed to have more effect on Peter than on Martin. The two of them parted, and Peter turned resolutely away in the direction of the promenade.

A middle-aged married couple wagged disapproving heads.

"Some of them can't keep off it. A

couple of drinks and they're away."

"It's worse in Margate."

The sea bubbled and seethed in a spasm of skittish energy around the girders of the pier. The wood beneath Brigid's feet trembled. She took Martin's hand. They gave Peter a good start and then made their own way landwards.

On Sunday there was the usual teatime session. Mrs Hemming was taciturn. Martin tried to persuade her to bring out the wedding cake and show it to Brigid. When Brigid added her pleas, Mrs Hemming lashed out:

"Are you sure you still need it?"

Suppose, thought Brigid, I were to pick up her best teapot and throw it through the window and then run amok through the hotel and scare the daylights out of her guests: Oh, to horrify Mrs Hemming, who loved her hotel to be so quiet, who had fitted padded doors to the television lounge so that its mumble should not disturb guests who thought and felt and suffered as she did, and who took every precaution to muffle kitchen noises, the sound of lavatories flushing, and the chatter of staff in the corridors.

Suppose I were to stamp and have tantrums, say I've had just about enough . . .

No. She must stay calm. They would have their wedding and their two weeks in Malta far from these petty irritations, and could come back and close their own front door on other people's moods and tempers and twitches.

It was just a matter of holding on and not snapping.

"I can't stand it," said Mrs Hemming abruptly. "It's no good. I've got to speak out."

Brigid's good resolves splintered. "If you're still fretting about my grandfather . . . look, the murder wasn't my idea. Nor the publicity we've been getting. Surely you're not still holding that against me? And as for Peter Blythe, it's not my doing that he came to Lurgate."

"You seem very partial to him. Going out for drives, and fixing things behind Martin's back, I don't doubt."

"Fixing things?"

"Martin's not going to be robbed." Mrs Hemming choked on a hysterical sob. "I won't have it."

"Mum." Martin was terribly calm, with a warning anger just below the surface. "There's never been any question of robbing me. I'm not marrying Brigid for her money. Just because this chap rolls up out of the blue and says he's old Walter's grandson, or Serafina's, or whoever . . . "

"Oh, he's Serafina's grandson all right, I reckon. Not much mistake about that."

Brigid gasped. "But I thought you didn't believe . . . "

"Not at first. Just couldn't let myself. But it's no good blinking it, is it? Only that's not the point."

"Mum, you've got to stop this. I won't have you carrying on in this way." Martin's anger reached the surface.

"I don't believe Walter Blythe ever did marry Serafina," said his mother. "Not properly." She pointed at him. "*You're* Walter Blythe's grandson — his proper one! You're the one who was let down . . . *you're* the one who ought to inherit."

8

TO Nell the whole thing appeared to be moving rapidly into the realm of farce. Hastily summoned to Mrs Hemming's neat, cramped sitting room, she found her attention straying from this new extravagance to the sober reality of the darkly patterned wallpaper, the lumpy old radio set and the glass-fronted corner cupboard. She had to make an effort to concentrate. Arthur would expect a coherent report from her.

He had been called away an hour earlier by the vicar of a village four miles inland who had asked if there was a chance of a chat with him before or after evensong. Or, if not today, tomorrow. The subject was a Georgian house threatened by what the vicar considered to be an unnecessary safety measure mooted by the R.D.C. They wanted to pull the house down because it was a danger to traffic on a sharp corner and was liable to collapse. The vicar thought the danger lay in the traffic and the corner itself, not in the house. He sought expert advice with which to confound the Philistines.

Even in a time of stress like the present one, such an appeal could not fail to bring Arthur galloping to the rescue. He had set out before this fresh development in the Blythe saga was reported by Brigid. Nell had to stand in for him.

Concentrate. She must concentrate.

Mrs Hemming was saying: "I've already told you that I accept him being Serafina's grandson. I'm not arguing that. But Peter *Blythe* — I don't reckon he's got the right to call himself that. Serafina didn't come to this country till five years after Walter Blythe married my mother."

"You mean" — Nell was still incapable of formulating the relevant questions, and Brigid was doing it for her — "Walter Blythe was your father?"

"Yes."

"You were alive, then, when he came to Lurgate and went into partnership with Victor Johnson?"

"No."

"No, of course not." Brigid thought this over. "Everyone would have known about

146

you. We'd have heard before this. But if he had one wife, and then brought Serafina here, didn't people . . . "

"My mother didn't come to Lurgate with him," said Mrs Hemming stiffly. "He . . . he'd left her before he set up in business here. She didn't know where he'd gone."

Nell shook herself into alertness. She said: "Then how could he be your father?"

"She found him again. And he'd had enough of Serafina by then, and between them he and my mother started to make plans. And when he knew I was on the way," she said with a defiant jerk of the head, "he decided to leave."

Nell found herself looking at Martin's white, incredulous face.

He said: "Mum, are you sure you know what you're saying? You've never told me a word of this."

"Any more than my mother told *me*, till she felt it was right I ought to know. Oh, I'm sure of what I'm saying, all right."

Now that she was launched, Mrs Hemming wasted no words. There were

147

no frills, no embellishments. Not like the sideboard runner with its tassels, not like her lace doilies, not like the bobbles on her cushions and the blue chenille tablecloth which, she had once told Nell, had been her mother's favourite.

"My mother," she said, "married Walter Blythe when he hadn't a penny to his name. It was in North Wales, some way inland from Pwllheli. Lonely in those days, and they didn't have much contact with the outside world. If someone went off into England, it could be the last you'd ever hear of them. The country's shrunk a lot since then."

Walter Blythe had worked in the slate quarries and then set up in a small way as a jobbing builder. He was shrewd and energetic, and he had a flair — he was a cocky man, more ambitious and more inventive than most of the folk among whom he had been brought up. The valley wouldn't hold him. He grew restless. He made one or two forays out of Wales into the English Midlands in search of brighter opportunities. His wife was not anxious to move. They had belonged to this one community for ages, and she disliked the idea of change. People who went away tended to get lost. Awful things could happen to them. Men who went off to Liverpool promised they'd be back rolling in money; but a lot of them were never seen again, and very few of them ever brought any money back to their parents or sent as much as a letter to say they were all right. And as for those who went off to London — well, it wasn't much better than going to sea and off to the ends of the earth.

When Walter Blythe left the valley, he left on his own. It started out ostensibly as one of his little sorties, and his wife waited apprehensively for him to come back and tell her about some wild new scheme he'd hatched while he was away. But this time he didn't come back.

"But surely she made some effort to find him?" protested Nell. She couldn't imagine sitting demurely at home and bowing her head to fate if Arthur failed to return from a trip one day.

"It's easy enough to talk," said Mrs Hemming. "Nowadays there's radio, and police all over the place, and newspapers printing descriptions, and you've got to have an insurance card if you want to get a job and there's all kinds of courts you can dash into and ask for maintenance or for someone to get their hands on husbands and find out what they're up to . . . But not then. And a country girl wouldn't know where to start. She couldn't just set off on her own.Of course she asked — she got the local minister to do what he could for her, and she waited to hear, and she thought perhaps Walter was in trouble and he'd be back sooner or later. But he didn't come. So she went to work, sewing and dressmaking, and got herself a bit of money saved, and when she'd had enough of people in the valley looking at her and making fun of her, she worked up the courage to get out and start looking for her husband."

"I'm not sure I'd have wanted him after all that," said Brigid.

"There wasn't anything else she could think of." Mrs Hemming spoke awkwardly. It was not easy for her to speak of obsessive physical or emotional passions. A rough red stain seeped up into her cheeks. "She . . . always had him on her mind. She used to tell me what fun he was, how you couldn't resist him even when he'd let you down dreadfully — and although she had plenty to do to keep herself alive, and a young woman couldn't move about as easily as she does nowadays, she made a sort of . . . well, a sort of programme, I suppose you'd say . . . of looking for him. And in the end she found him. He hadn't even changed his name. He just used to expect to get away with things. It was easier then."

Mrs Hemming shook her head, but Nell detected an unmistakable note of reluctant admiration in her voice.

She said: "But you never knew him, yourself?"

"How could I?" Now there was the crack of accusation snapping across the room. "My mother and father were going to forget the past and start all over again. They met secretly, and . . . and he fell in love with her all over again. I was conceived. But only a few weeks later, when he was so pleased — my mother told me he'd been longing to have a child, and for all her looks and the rest of it Serafina hadn't been any good . . . "

"She did produce a son in the end," Nell pointed out.

"But who was the boy's father?"

"Well, naturally, one imagines . . . "

Nell blinked with a new uncertainty and sat back. The lower sash of the window was open and the trees a few yards away were rustling coolly and refreshingly. It would be so nice to get out of this room and go for a walk to clear her head.

"Naturally?" Mrs Hemming echoed scornfully. "Oh, it was easy enough for her to make out her son was Walter Blythe's. Nobody was going to ask any questions, the way she told it. But just you try tracking down the dates and getting them all exact, and there's no telling — you might get a different picture. Serafina could have married someone else for all we know, the minute she got back home. Or she might have met someone on the way there and . . . well, you know what they say about these hot-blooded Italians. From all I've heard of her, she was the flighty type. Could have got herself into trouble. So Luigi comes along, and she makes out his father was my father."

"You're saying this is all a put-up job by Peter Blythe?"

"Calling himself Blythe, indeed! He inherited all his grandmother's bits and pieces and dreamed up a fine story that'd make you break your heart over him. Oh, it's a nice story, I'll grant you. But the one *I'm* telling you is the truth."

Brigid looked unhappily at Martin. Nell felt for the two of them. Their wedding preparations ought never to have been spoilt by that earlier shadow; now the darkness was thickening.

There must be some light somewhere. "So your mother found Walter Blythe here in Lurgate," she prompted. "And then . . . "

"Well, they couldn't stay on here, could they? He had to take her away and start again somewhere else. And it suited him. The way my mother told it, he was ready to move on anyway. He was restless again and needed a new . . . er . . . "

"Kick?" said Brigid.

"Stimulus," said Mrs Hemming aloofly.

"So" — Nell carefully picked her way — "he *could* have embezzled that money. It could have been him after

153

all, getting the cash together ready to clear out."

"I don't believe that. My mother never said anything like that. And I don't think she'd have gone along with it."

"She didn't have to know. He'd have done it without telling her a word. And just when he was all set . . . "

"Then your father-in-law caught him at it and murdered him? I don't think so, Mrs Johnson. It doesn't make sense. I may not be all that bright, but even I can see that. Why not just expose him, have him taken to court and maybe sent to jail — get rid of him legally? Victor Johnson could still have taken over the firm, all above board, and got the money back to help him run it. No — he wanted my father out of the way. That's the only explanation. *He* fixed the books, and *he* murdered my father. He didn't know about my mother — nobody did. But he had to have my father out of the way so that there'd be nobody to challenge his story about the money. And nobody to share the profits with any more. Two birds with one stone."

Nell was silent. If there was a more

rational solution, she didn't know it.

Mrs Hemming went on.

When Walter Blythe had disappeared and the news of the embezzlement came out, Eiluned Blythe sadly believed that it was the same old story all over again. Walter's feet had been itching to move: he longed for the change they had talked about; but once more it was to be Walter on his own, not Walter with her. He was leaving Serafina, as promised; but once again he was leaving Eiluned, too. She ought to have known.

He had been giving her money, but now the money stopped. She had to leave Lurgate. She went back to Wales, but not to her own village. They would have asked too many questions, and the arrival of a baby wouldn't have helped matters. She could honestly say it was Walter's, but then there would be the inevitable question: Where was Walter this time? She couldn't face contempt again; couldn't face either laughter or callous disbelief. She went to a coastal town not unlike Lurgate — a town which in later years was to draw in more and more visitors from Liverpool and Manchester, a town where it was possible to be anonymous.

Mrs Hemming remembered her mother's struggles. As she grew up she had helped her. Eiluned Blythe put it about that she was a widow and told this story to her daughter also. She worked as a cook in one of the hotels when she was able to leave the little girl, Betty, on her own: she was allowed to live in with Betty on condition that she took a much reduced wage.

It was not until Betty was about to marry that she was told the truth. She heard the full story, because her mother considered that she was now an adult woman: she was about to get married, so she was now worthy of confidences.

Betty married a good man. "And we had a good son," she said fiercely, glaring at Martin as though daring him to deny it. Her mother died during the war, and after the war the Hemmings decided to set up in the hotel business themselves. They worked as cook and under-manager in a large hotel on the Wirral for two years, and then saw the advertisement for Fernrock Hotel in Lurgate. It was not the only advertisement they answered, but the name of Lurgate tempted Mrs Hemming. She wanted to see the place and live in it and perhaps, one day, find out something of what had really happened.

But she never told her husband any of the background story, and never gave her son the slightest hint.

"I can't see what all the fuss was about." Martin found his voice at last. He spoke shakily, like a small boy on the verge of tears. "All this moral twitching — it's pitiful. Why not tell the truth from the start? There was no shame in it so far as your mother was concerned. Or you yourself. Why this . . . this blanket of stuffy convention?"

"You young folk today are so hard. You talk about anything at all, without as much as a blush. It wasn't like that for us."

"It was all right to lie, then? You could twist the truth any way you liked so long as it kept up appearances. But if you told the truth there was no hope for you — no charity, no understanding?"

His mother was silent for a moment and then said grudgingly: "Maybe some things are better today. In some ways. But only in some ways, mind you."

"She didn't think of speaking to the others — to my grandfather — and proving who she was, and asking them to help her?" asked Brigid.

"How could she? She was so ashamed. He'd left her once. Now he'd left her again, and she was going to have his baby — me. And it looked as though he'd stolen a small fortune. She could never have brought herself to utter a word."

"It's funny," mused Brigid. "It's . . . well, don't you see — it's almost the same story."

"The same?"

"As Peter's. Shame . . . pride . . . running off and hiding in a place where you wouldn't be heard of again. Not by people in Lurgate, anyway. Telling people you're a widow and going on living like that for the rest of your days. It's such a weird parallel — your mother and Serafina."

Nell was staring abstractedly at the open window. Startlingly, Peter Blythe's face was framed in the opening. His hands were on the sill, and his toes must be rammed firmly again the bricks below.

He said: "Yes, it is odd, I think. I am fascinated. *Tema con variazione*, eh?"

Mrs Hemming let out a little shriek, but her fear changed swiftly to towering indignation. She got up. Before she could reach the window, which she clearly had every intention of slamming down — preferably on Peter's fingers — he braced himself, thrust upwards, and toppled sideways into the room.

"But we do know, don't we," he said, "which is the original theme and which the variation?"

9

THEY sat on their favourite bench in the shelter of the white, squat lighthouse on the promontory. The wind was rising, penning the Easter Monday crowds in the town itself. It smacked boisterously against the glass panels of the pier pavilion, against the hotels and boarding houses, and against the lighthouse.

Brigid and Martin turned towards each other to save their words from being snatched away like torn twigs. But Martin could not meet her gaze. He looked away again, tight-lipped, out over the flecks of light and darkness on the waves. A ragged tongue of black rocks divided the sands into two ochre bays. Water seethed round the rocks, tugging at them, pulling them slowly below the foam.

Martin narrowed his eyes as though it was absolutely essential that he should see the farthest tip of rock at the very last second before it was engulfed.

"Please," said Brigid. "Please, Martin. Don't just sit there scowling."

"Sorry." But the scowl remained as stubborn ridges in his forehead. "I've got this feeling. Only it's not feeling at all. Numbness. I want to . . . to *do* something, but I'm winded. Having this sprung on me — on us!"

Brigid reached for his hand. It was as cold as though he had been holding it defiantly out to be chilled by the wind.

"It doesn't make any difference to us."

"I'll take damned good care it doesn't," he said fiercely. Just as fiercely he said: "Oh, you know darned well we can't just pretend all those things weren't said. My mother going on about your family, and that dirty little creep wanting things from your family . . . "

"We came here," she reminded him, "to talk about pictures for the flat, and bookcases and things."

But inevitably they talked about Peter Blythe.

"I ought to have bashed his face in."

"You think that would have settled everything? Tidied up the loose ends, answered all the questions, sent him away chastened?"

"At least it'd have shut him up for a while."

The sound of Peter's voice was still in Brigid's head — a sour, harsh sound as he set about demolishing Mrs Hemming's claims by scorn rather than sweet reason. She had shown them a locket holding a photograph of a man and woman, their heads close together. The faces were tiny, and the hand-tinting of the picture had faded over the years. One face was undoubtedly Blythe's; the other, she swore, as her mother's. The locket had been handed on to her by her mother. Peter inspected the picture and shook his head knowingly. The woman, he conjectured, could just possibly have been his grandmother, wearing a different hair style, but he didn't really believe even that: it was more likely that the picture was a clumsy fake. If the face was really that of Mrs Hemming's mother, it had been added to the original.

Mrs Hemming had raged at him. Peter had shrugged. Was this the best she had to offer?

Triumphantly she produced her birth certificate. What was this insufferable foreigner going to make of *that*, then? Her parents were shown on the form as Walter Edwin Blythe and Eiluned Blythe formerly Jenkins.

"Do you think I'm boasting about being the daughter of a man like that?" Mrs Hemming had cried. "But you can't deny it. There it is, in black and white."

Peter had airily waved it aside. "Anyone they can show the pieces of paper." Was Blythe such an uncommon name in England? Who was to say that this was the same Walter Blythe? Even if it was, since the man was dead at the time of the child's birth and only the mother could have applied for the certificate, what was to stop her inventing anything she wished about the father?

They had tried to explain to him that the birth certificate could not have been made out in such a form unless Eiluned Jenkins' own marriage certificate, establishing her as the wife of Walter Blythe, had been produced to the registrar. Still Peter infuriatingly shook his head, dismissing anything he did not wish to believe was true.

Martin continued to stare down at the water. "I've had it out with Mum. She can't come up with much, apart from that certificate. I wish . . . I wish I didn't have to believe her."

"But she's sure it's genuine. Anyone can see that."

He allowed himself a wintry smile. "Oh, she's sure, all right. But for all we know, our precious Pietro has a further selection of jolly tricks to pull out of the hat."

"Maybe he was more shaken than he liked to show. Maybe he'll clear off now, and not come back."

"Oh, he won't give in. That's the awful thing, you know: whatever this whole business may add up to in the end, he's genuinely convinced that he's in the right. He may be a rotten bastard, a sharp boy, out for all he can get — but he does honestly believe that he's entitled to it."

"Your mother believes just as strongly."

"Yes, but she hasn't got much to offer. Against *him* . . . "

Brigid found herself instinctively taking Mrs Hemming's side. "What would you expect her to offer? She admitted she hadn't got many souvenirs. When her mother and Blythe were married, they were pretty poor. If he did get his hands on any money, he doesn't seem the type who'd have spent it on his wife. Later, when he was prosperous and he had a flashy Sicilian wife to show off, things were different. He never gave your grandmother much to remember him by except your mother."

"It's been hard on her."

Brigid could imagine that. It had always been hard, but now her resentment must be near to boiling over. On behalf of her dead mother rather than herself, Mrs Hemming had hated the memory of Walter Blythe. Settling in Lurgate, she had resented the Johnsons, who were living on a scale which she felt her own son was entitled to.

"Your mother and father" — Martin crashed into her thoughts — "are positive by now that my mother shoved me at you, so that at least one of us could get something back out of the carve-up."

"Did *you* feel that you were being pushed at me?"

"No."

"That's all right, then. And it couldn't make any difference now, anyway — not the way I feel about you."

Martin at last turned towards her again and looked into her eyes. He didn't speak. Brigid said, with difficulty, not wanting to coax him but needing to have him reassure her:

"And you? You're not sorry you met me?"

"Darling." His hand had warmed in her grasp. His fingers curled over hers, gripping them painfully. "Let's talk about pictures," he said, "and bookcases — and things."

"Things."

"Such as being in love. I love you very much. Love, and pictures, and carpets and bookcases and . . . and being with you. It sounds a bit muddled . . . "

"No," said Brigid. "Not muddled at all. The way you put it, it makes wonderful sense. Particularly the bit about being with me. And as for the rest, it doesn't make any difference to us." She must say it over and over again so they would both believe it. "If my mother gets niggly, let her. If she and your mother get together . . . but no, maybe they won't even speak to each other now. Pride . . . "

"Pride!" he exploded. "Look where it got the rest of them! All that agonising all over the shop, fifty years ago. Everyone stiff-necked and holy and proud — proud of money, the firm, the family name, the right to self-righteous poverty. Pride? You can keep it."

The wind was veering round and snarling at them. They got up and walked past the lighthouse.

"If it comes to pride," said Martin more quietly, "what about mine? Hearing all this about my own background. Parents, grandparents, all our ancestors all the way back to William the Bastard — pity we can't blot out the lot."

They parted outside Fernrock Hotel. Martin went indoors. The trees up here amplified the roar of the wind. A holiday-maker staying in one of the upper rooms of the hotel must, thought Brigid, have some of the sensations of being aboard a cruise liner in a choppy sea. Enjoyment would depend on whether or not you were a good sailor.

She went down the slope to the promenade and walked briskly towards the main shopping streets of the town. A few hardy souls had ventured out in the rising gale, determined to boast that they loved the sea breezes. Below, long ranks of frothing ripples advanced over the now submerged rocks with a throaty rasp.

Suddenly she realised that a young man had fallen into step beside her.

Peter said: "An interesting fantasy, wasn't it?"

"I don't think we have anything to say to each other."

"Ah. This is the cold English disdain, yes? The haughty upper lip, I think."

"You think wrong. It's just that I'd sooner not . . . "

"Interesting," he repeated. "The Mrs Hemming, she goes through my luggage in her hotel — oh, yes, but of course it was her — and she has the pieces to make a pattern. She makes up such a beautiful story for herself. It is so like my own story, yes? Suspicious, I think. So like."

"They can't both be true," said Brigid flatly.

"That is so. Ah" — Peter spread his arms — "if only the characters were all of royal blood, such a libretto Verdi would have adored!"

Brigid said: "I really must hurry. I have some shopping to do."

"What do you think she hopes to gain by her silly little comedy?"

Brigid's head was spinning. She had already had enough of this — with all of them, with Martin, and now with Peter. Treading the same ground over and over again . . . stumbling through the maze, punch-drunk, fed up.

But she had to grapple with it. Sooner or later she had to find her way out of the maze.

"That birth certificate," she said. "It has Walter Blythe's name on it as Mrs Hemming's father."

"I said it meant nothing. Still I say it means nothing."

"I'd say it meant a lot."

"The registrar," Brigid insisted, "wouldn't enter that name without seeing a valid marriage certificate between Walter

Blythe and the mother."

"A forgery, then. It is of no consequence." He shrugged. "It is easy to forge documents."

"Not in this country, it isn't."

"No? I tell you, lovely Brigid, anywhere it is easy. If you know the people, it is easy." He nodded and smiled as though in appreciation of his opponent's tactics — an appreciation which would not alter his determination to win. "I do not know why it was done. There is a lot we do not know, I think. But one thing I know — I know the truth. The truth of myself, and what I must have."

They waited to cross the road by the island of flowerbeds from which radiated streets climbing steeply into the town. Brigid looked straight ahead, wondering how she could shake him off.

He said: "Now I think I must find another hotel."

She could not suppress a wry smile. "I don't imagine you're exactly a welcome guest."

"Perhaps I am stabbed to death in my bed."

"In Lurgate?"

"There are no deaths in Lurgate? No passion, no killing? I think it is dull. I think I go away."

"Away?"

He laughed. "You are so anxious I go?" Before she could stammer an excuse, he went on: "And you will come with me?"

"Certainly not."

"I ask you to think about it."

"Where were you proposing to take me?" She made it as sarcastic as possible.

"We find out when we get there. That is the only way to travel."

"You fancy me as a useful accomplice? You hope to keep working on my father through me — keep draining the firm?"

His smile stayed on his lips but hardened. As they crossed the road he walked a step ahead of her as though gallantly to clear the way, and turned to meet her on the opposite kerb. He crinkled his eyes up into what was meant to be an endearing grin. As a small boy he must have been irresistible. No doubt his grandmother had spoilt him — the only man left in the family, in a land where, Brigid had heard or read somewhere, large families were the rule and sons were idolised. But the eyes were not childish now and they were not endearing. They were calculating and far too old for his years.

She stood still, wanting him to go away. Whichever direction he took, she would take a different one.

At the top of the steps which led to the shore, two workmen in green Corporation uniform were unloading deckchairs from a cart. The canvas, faded by earlier seasons, billowed in the breeze. Nobody was sitting on the shore today, but the date and time for the supply of extra deck-chairs had been decreed by the Corporation weeks ago and the routine had to be observed. Optimistically the men humped the chairs down the steps.

Brigid knew everything about Lurgate. All its nuances, all its moods. She could tell a visitor from a day tripper, a resident from even the most discreet, quiet holidaymaker. She knew almost too much about the place. Escape was a tempting prospect. But not with Peter.

"You know what I think?" he said. "I think maybe your Mrs Hemming's mother killed my grandfather."

"What a ridiculous . . . "

"But yes."

"One minute you hardly believe in her existence, the next you're dreaming up murder plots about her."

"I do not believe in her as my grandfather's wife, no. But his mistress, perhaps? And she find that he has had enough, that his wife is more beautiful. And he and his wife are going to leave the country, and the mistress she grows jealous."

"Then why wouldn't she have murdered your grandmother rather than your grandfather?"

He nodded bland acknowledgment of this point. "It is a puzzle, I agree. So much is still a puzzle. But I think . . . "

His voice trailed away. Brigid had not been looking at him. Even while they talked she had been deliberately looking away, implying that she wanted a quick end to the conversation, that she was already on her way somewhere else. Now she glanced at him.

Peter stood rigid for a moment. He stared. He could not have been stricken more stiff and dumb if one of the passing trippers had snatched off a paper hat to reveal the face of Medusa.

Before Brigid knew what was happening, he came abruptly to life. His hand grabbed her arm and he dragged her unceremoniously up the nearest street.

"Stop it! Just a minute . . . !"

They stumbled under the green metal awning of a row of shops which had altered little since Victorian times. Peter obviously had no idea where he was. He looked blankly up at the shop names, and then down the street. A bulging, untrimmed privet hedge leaned out over a low wall and obscured the view of the promenade.

Brigid said: "What on earth . . . ?"

"Ten thousand pounds," he said breathlessly. He gabbled a few words which must have been Italian, then gulped and made himself speak English again, slowly. "What you think ten thousand pounds it means today? Ten thousand pounds from . . . from 1913, I mean."

"Haven't a clue."

"The money they say my grandfather stole. But he did not steal." He glanced down towards the promenade and began to urge Brigid further up the street. They stopped on a corner, where a long arc of roadway carried traffic away inland. "We know it was not my grandfather. *Your* grandfather — it was he who stole. And stole my grandfather's life also."

Brigid tugged her arm free. "What are you ranting on about? And what's all the rush?"

"You think maybe your father settle for fifty thousand pounds? Fifty thousand and then he is rid of me. Very reasonable."

"Settle? You mean you want to get out?"

"I think I do not live here."

"Your claim won't stand up to Martin's," she challenged. "That's why you're in such a flap. That's what you're afraid of."

"Is nonsense. But I do not stay here. I would not be liked." There was no humour whatsoever left in his smile. "And for me, I like to be liked. This is a cold place. Me, I find it very cold."

He gave a genuine shiver.

Brigid said: "I wouldn't advise you to try and blackmail my father."

"Who is talking of blackmail? I talk

about a settlement. Man to man. The truth. We all know the truth. You speak for me — you ask your father, you find out for me?"

"No. You must see him yourself."

Peter came to the house that same evening. He was closeted with Brigid's father for twenty minutes. When he left, he was humming to himself.

Brigid waited for her father to emerge. His face was pale and drained. Her mother, waiting just as tautly as Brigid, went to his side. Brigid felt suddenly and absurdly weepy as she saw how close they were. For the first time in her life she felt almost shut out; and in the same flash saw what it meant to be truly husband and wife.

She said: "Daddy, what did he say?"

"Same sort of thing as before. Only more of it."

"You didn't give him any money, did you? You didn't let him . . . "

"Brigid." Her mother was sharp, really thrusting her away. "Your father's very tired. We'll talk about it when he feels like talking about it."

"I only wanted to know what happened."

The next day, Martin also wanted to know what happened. It must have been something big, something climactic — because Peter had not returned to the hotel that night.

"He was talking of moving out," said Brigid. "He felt it wasn't quite the right place for him. I expect he's found somewhere else."

"Without luggage? His bags are still in his room. We've had a look. And he hasn't paid his bill."

Thinking wretchedly that her father must have been pressured into giving Peter money, that Peter must have been out on a delirious spending spree, Brigid said: "He'll be back. I'm sure of it. He'll pay his bill and collect his bags, and . . . "

"And?"

"Oh, I don't know. I just don't know."

But Peter didn't come back. Two days later the luggage was still there, the bill was still unpaid, and there was no sign of Peter.

10

THE clatter of dustbin lids jarred Nell awake. After the first crash, coming from a house some distance away, there was a moment's lull; then the wind rose again and skittishly moved a lid down a garden path or across what might be a patch of crazy paving.

There was a faint slithering noise overhead, followed by a crunch somewhere below the window. A slate must have come off the roof. There would probably be more by morning.

Nell buried her right ear in the pillow. It was no use: she was already wide awake.

Arthur muttered in his sleep and hunched closer.

There was a buffet against the house, then a sigh. Nell waited tensely for the next gust, trying to predict it and fall into the rhythm. There was no rhythm. The wind was unpredictable. It stormed, moaned, whispered.

She turned over.

The wind became the insidious voice of Peter Blythe, needling her, demanding answers she couldn't give. She told him to go away and tried to find a way of convincing him that there was nothing here for him.

But he *had* gone, hadn't he? It was the manner of his going that was so worrying. She must call him back. He must start all over again, do it properly, leaving everything tidy. As soon as she allowed herself to think of the word 'tidy', Nell found that Mrs Hemming was in the scene, fussy and meticulous.

If she went to sleep now, they would both follow her into a dream.

It was just as it had been, years ago, when she was learning to drive. Her foot twitched, she went over and over a mistake — even a possible mistake, a misinterpretation — and she wanted to reverse everything, go back to the beginning and then set off properly, flawlessly. On the edge of sleep her foot used to slip off the clutch and she would be jolted forward in bed.

"Huh . . . mm . . . what's 'at?" Arthur

grunted now, just as he had done then.

Peter Blythe snickered.

Come back and explain yourself, she said in her head, and then clear off for good. Let me tell you what I think of you, and then go.

Arthur groped for the edge of the sheet and tugged it over him.

Nell was thankful when the morning light filtered through the parted curtains and tinted the end of the bed. She got up early and had drunk two cups of coffee by the time Arthur and Brigid came down to breakfast.

In the middle of the meal, there was a telephone call from the Borough Surveyor. He wanted Arthur's professional opinion. There had been a nasty subsidence of the cliff below Fernrock Hotel during the night, and some urgent work might be needed. Could they meet there in half an hour?

"I'll drive you," said Nell.

Arthur looked mildly surprised. "No need to bother, love."

"You've got so much on your mind just now. You don't concentrate on the road at the best of times. I hate to think what you'd be like today."

Arthur looked even more surprised. "You know, I'm perfectly capable . . . "

"Besides," said Nell finally, "I feel like getting out."

Arthur and Brigid exchanged wry, speculative glances. Nell was tempted to snap at both of them and tell them to wipe that silly expression off their faces. She restrained herself. Arthur would almost certainly have said that *she* was not in a fit state to drive the car.

They went slowly along the ridge. Neighbours were sweeping up fragments of slate or examining garage and outhouse roofs.

The wind had dropped. Below, the sea was oily and sullen. It appeared threatening rather than restful, as though waiting for the wind to revive so that they could launch a concerted attack on the heavy blocks shoring up the promenade.

Nell drove towards the bluff. From this angle, approaching it from the side, Fernrock did look precariously exposed. *Ideal situation, magnificent sea vista* . . . The advertisements were accurate enough; but when a storm raged perhaps

181

the situation was not quite so ideal.

She drew up on the gravel before the hotel entrance. They got out and walked to the edge of the terraced gardens.

The fissure down the slope had widened into an alarming gash. Boulders and long, deadly slivers of rock had been clawed from the cliff by the wind. Some were poised, some had wrecked the flowerbeds; others had cascaded down the steep decline. The low wall at the foot of the gardens had shattered under the impact and was fragmented all over the promenade. Rubble was scattered far across the road and on to the beach. From where they stood, Nell and Arthur could see the stumpy, remote figures of policemen erecting barriers and emergency traffic signs across the promenade.

Hankey, the Borough Surveyor, was crouching over the gash. He saw Arthur and beckoned him down.

"Do be careful," said Nell.

He patted her shoulder, his attention already on the job ahead, and strode down the nearest path. The two men went into a huddle.

She wondered what they would have to do. The opening was a great wound in the cliff, its earthy sides as brown as dried blood down the green slope. Nell had an incongruous vision of giant machines stitching the edges together. But in reality they would have to fill up the gap, strengthen it, perhaps shore up the whole cliff. One corner of the hotel was dangerously near the top end of the fissure.

There was an awful lot of débris to be removed; an awful lot of strengthening to be done; and an awful lot of money involved.

Arthur and Hankey prowled and sprang about like clumsy mountain goats who had lost the knack. They prodded and scratched at the ground as though intent on making the whole cliff subside.

"Good morning, Mrs Johnson."

Martin had come from the hotel. He stood beside Nell, his gaze following hers down the ravaged garden.

"Day off?" she said.

"I rang the lab and begged some free time. A few of the guests are getting crotchety, and Mum's in a bit of a state."

"I don't blame her."

They walked slowly down the path until it swerved left and disintegrated into the gash. Martin stooped and examined the farther wall. He pointed.

"Interesting root formation. I wonder how . . . ?"

He lowered himself to the edge and swung his feet in. His head was just below the level of the ground. Nell visualised the earth closing in and annihilating him without warning.

"Do be careful, Martin."

He touched the tendrils of the root and splayed them out gently between his fingers.

From the slope above came a faint rustling sound. It was like the mutter of a stream over pebbles; but there was no water here.

Nell looked round.

A boulder was trundling down from the trees on the ridge, setting a cascade of stones and dust in motion. They rasped against each other and gathered speed. A small avalanche poured into the trench and came rumbling down.

Martin sprang back, but his feet

scrabbled against the side and he was stuck for a moment with his arms and shoulders over the edge, holding tight but unable to move. Nell got her hands under his arms and pulled. Martin's toes dug into the earth and thrust away. He rolled clear as the boulder racketed past.

The skyline reeled. Against it, Nell had a blurred picture of the windbreak of trees and of a woman's shape against the light. The figure crouched and hurried into shadow. It was gone so quickly, and she was so dazed, that it could all have been a trick of the light.

"Arthur!" It was her own voice, shouting a warning. "Arthur ... look out!"

"It's all right, Mrs Johnson."

She straightened up, and Martin got up beside her. They could see that Arthur and Hankey were already standing clear, letting the rubble slow and settle, choking part of the gash.

Arthur came up the slope. The Borough Surveyor toiled after him, musing pessimistically with his head sunk between his shoulders.

"Arthur, that might have ... it's not

safe, you mustn't . . . "

"Thank you, Mrs Johnson," Martin was saying, but she hardly heard him.

A woman came down the path. Nell stiffened. The shape and the movement brought back into focus her brief memory of the woman in the trees, scuttling away after the boulder had started to move.

Mrs Hemming said: "What is it now? Whatever's happening?"

Nell stared at her. She said: "Was that you . . . up there, in the trees?"

"Me? I've just come from the kitchen."

"Nell" — Arthur's hand was on her arm — "what's the matter?"

"Nothing. That is, I thought I saw . . . in the trees, just before . . . but it couldn't have been."

Couldn't have been, she said to herself. Mrs Hemming wasn't going to roll huge chunks of rock down on her only son.

"Nell," said Arthur: "go home."

"But I . . . "

"Martin, would it be too much of a nuisance for you to drive Mrs Johnson home and then bring the car back here and leave it for me?"

"Of course not, sir. A small recompense

for having my life saved!"

"Arthur, I'm perfectly capable of driving myself home."

"And then how do I get the car back here?" His hand moved up to her shoulder. He kissed her and said firmly: "Go home, my pet. Run off — before your shivers and shakes bring the whole place down round our ears."

Nell allowed herself to be taken home.

At lunchtime Arthur was grave, his mind utterly wrapped up in the problems of Fernrock. "It's going to be a very tricky job," he said. "Very dicey." The Borough Surveyor was talking of evacuating the hotel. Some of the guests were already leaving of their own accord. Mrs Hemming was telephoning the other Lurgate hotels to find alternative accommodation.

"Poor Betty," said Nell. "On top of everything else!"

"It never rains but what it pours."

"Perhaps I ought to come over and see if I can help."

"Leave it till the late afternoon," said Arthur. "Then we can come back together."

She knew that he had hardly tasted his

lunch. He was drawn back to the work in hand — eager to be at it again.

The afternoon dragged. At half past five she went over to Fernrock and watched while four men with tapes and little hammers and painted poles and sextants swarmed over the terraces. At least, she thought they were using sextants: she had always been interested in Arthur's work but had been careful not to pick up surface technicalities or jargon which would irritate rather than please him.

At six o'clock Arthur said: "Another half-hour yet. Why not go in and breathe sweetness and light over Mrs H? Wasn't that the purpose of the visit?"

"Don't be too long."

"I'll come and break the bad news over the carpet as soon as I can."

Bracing herself against the inevitable antagonism, Nell went into the hotel.

"A fine kettle of fish," said Mrs Hemming.

Martin put four glasses and a bottle of sherry on the table. He was taking out the cork when the door opened and a pink-cheeked girl peeped round it.

"Mrs Hemming — sorry, but there's

two more making a fuss. And some others want to go, but they're all right. I mean, they're being nice about it."

Mrs Hemming went out.

Martin poured three glasses of sherry and handed one to Nell.

"Quite a day," he said. "Three sorts of people. The ones who think it's our fault that the cliff has given way; those who are terribly nice about it, but want to get out just the same; and a few who say they're here and this is where they're going to stay — but what about a rebate?"

Mrs Hemming must have dealt brusquely with the latest batch of refugees. She was back in less than five minutes. She sat down, scowled at the sherry, drank some of it, and ran her little finger along her lips.

Without any preamble she said: "And on top of it all we had that reporter here. Snooping about, just like before. Hoping it'd be worse than it was, I'll be bound. He'd sooner there'd been a few folk crushed to death."

"If there's anything I can do," said Nell, "I do hope you'll . . . "

"And asking about that . . . that

Peter . . . Peter Blythe, he called himself."

"Asking what?"

"If there were any fresh developments. If he could have a talk with him."

Martin said: "You didn't tell me this."

"And I didn't tell him anything, either. What's it got to do with the papers? They've done enough mischief already."

"How did you get rid of him?" asked Nell quietly.

"Told him the chap was away. No idea where he'd gone. I said he wasn't in and I didn't know when he'd be back, and it was none of my business anyway."

Nell sensed that Betty Hemming was close to breaking point. Everything had gone wrong. Now the hotel was threatening to tumble about her in pieces. Soon she would ream, or throw something. Better if she could only break down and cry, and let someone else take over.

Martin leaned towards her, trying to force a smile. "Come on, Mum — you know you're the guilty party."

"Me?"

"You locked him in. Starved him to death, and then got rid of the body."

Mrs Hemming couldn't make even a pretence of treating this as a joke. "Locked in? He's still got the key with him, wherever he is. *And* he didn't pay his bill before he left. Didn't pay his bill — just walked off with the key." Her indignation was overflowing. That Peter should have walked off with the key of his room was somehow the worst affront of all.

Her anger was so spontaneous that it damped down a terrible doubt which had begun to flicker in Nell's mind.

Would Mrs Hemming have been capable of . . .

Well — of what?

She couldn't let herself frame it too bleakly.

Eliminating Peter Blythe. Eliminating. That was the nearest she would let herself approach it. It sounded more everyday and excusable, less violent, that way.

A telephone tinkled. It was the first time Nell had realised that there was a two-tone grey phone in the room, tucked way behind a photograph of a man in military uniform.

Mrs Hemming lifted the receiver. She

191

listened, said, "I'll come out," and put it down. "Somebody else," she said, her throat tight and strained.

She went out once more. When she returned, Arthur was with her. He had presumably wiped his feet at the door, but now trod very cautiously towards Nell as thought cowed into taking the minimum possible number of steps, and those on the tips of his toes.

"Well?" said Mrs Hemming.

Martin filled the fourth glass and passed it over. Arthur nodded his thanks. He drank and put the glass down with heavy deliberation.

"We'll need a few more tests. It's a matter of stabilising the cliff or the hotel. Or perhaps both. Or neither."

"How can it be neither?"

"There's been some subterranean erosion, by the look of it. Infiltration from the sea, round the far side of the bluff. There may be some caves under the hotel — or just some nasty holes. If the cliff can be held, we may be all right. But whatever happens, we'll have to check the hotel — foundations, walls, stresses, the lot."

"More money for the Johnsons," said Mrs Hemming.

Martin said: "Mum . . . !"

Arthur sipped at his drink again. He put his free hand in the small of his back and groaned slightly.

"But it'll be all right, won't it?" said Nell as confidently as possible. "It can all be straightened out somehow."

"All of it?" said Mrs Hemming. "The cliff — well, the Corporation'll have to do something about that, I grant you." She shook her head vigorously but without meaning. "And the hotel — well . . . "

"You're insured?"

"Of course I'm insured, but the mess — the loss of custom, the inconvenience . . . oh, it's too much. And anyway there are more important things, aren't there? Where's that Peter whatever-he-likes-to-call-himself? Where's he got to, that's what I want to know."

Martin looked levelly at Arthur and said: "Did you give him any money?"

Arthur hesitated.

"Well?" demanded Mrs Hemming. "Did you or didn't you?"

"Yes, I did."

"That little cheat. Liar. And you gave him money. Money that by rights belongs to . . . "

"Martin won't suffer," Arthur interrupted her. "I promise you that."

"How much? How much did you hand over?"

"That's my concern."

"By paying him," said Martin, "you were admitting that you accepted his claim."

"I saw no alternative. I didn't want a stand-up fight — legally, I mean."

"But he was a fraud," cried Mrs Hemming.

"Old Farnham was convinced."

"Old Farnham! A fat lot he remembers about anything. You handed over what he asked for" — she took up the refrain of money, money, money — "and with all that to play about with, he couldn't even pay his bill before he left."

If they were to demolish the hotel, thought Nell, half a century from now . . . or next week . . . would they find Peter Blythe's corpse in the cellar?

"I wanted the whole damned business settled," said Arthur fiercely. "Settled.

194

Written off. I don't know who was married and who wasn't married, and how many children and grandchildren there are scattered over the face of the earth. I do know I've had a bellyful of riddles. I've paid him off. I had to do it. And he's agreed not to worry us again."

"Probably having one hell of a time in London right now," said Martin.

His mother flailed to and fro as though on the verge of having a fit. "He'll fritter it away. All be gone in a few months. Then he'll be back for more. You mark my words: he'll be back."

"I wonder," said Martin. "I wonder if we'll ever see him again."

That infernal wind was rising again. It rattled the window and soughed round the side of the hotel. The room remained warm and stuffy. Mrs Hemming's anger, near to hysteria, added its own burning heat to the atmosphere.

Of course, Nell continued to reassure herself, Betty Hemming couldn't have had anything to do with the disappearance. Devotion to her son, yes. A puritanical fanaticism about those who had been wronged and those who had sinned.

195

Her obsessive neatness, her whole constricted background, a flame of terrible righteousness — yes, all right, all of that. But she wouldn't have killed. It wouldn't help; she must have known that.

But if Peter had come back, flourishing his cheque, telling her about it flamboyantly or slyly, saying he was off on his way to the bright lights, the good food and the drink and the world he could now afford to buy . . .

No. That sort of thing didn't happen among one's friends. Friends . . . Well, people close to one; people brought closer together by the impending marriage of their children.

The evening was darkening early. Storm clouds settled down over the bluff and along the promenade. Mrs Hemming got up to put the light on.

Some of the remaining guests hurried up from the seafront as rain spattered against the exposed side of the hotel. They could be heard trudging and mumbling across the hall.

"I don't know what to make of it all," said Mrs Hemming. "And all this just before the wedding."

This, too, had been in Nell's mind. She had not wanted to make the opening, but now that it was offered she could not resist saying:

"Do you think we ought to postpone it? Just until this is all settled."

"Postpone it?" said Martin.

"Just for the time being."

"No."

"When everyone's so upset . . . "

"I must say I'd feel easier in my mind," said Mrs Hemming.

Nell hastened to accept this alliance. "We're all so worried, and we really could do with a few weeks' breathing space while we sort things out — make sure of things."

Martin said: "I'm sure of everything that matters. So's Brigid."

"What I meant was, it would all be so much happier all round if we had absolutely everything else tidied up."

"You never did want Brigid to marry me, did you?" said Martin.

Arthur said: "Now, Martin . . . "

"It's true, isn't it? You've kept getting in the way, taking charge of things, making things difficult. Now you're grabbing at a last-minute excuse. Stay of execution, that sort of thing. Hoping for a last-minute reprieve?"

Nell said: "I only want what's best for Brigid. And with things as they are . . . "

She was interrupted by the dull but penetrating boom of the dinner gong. Again there was a shuffle of feet, a murmuring across the hall.

Mrs Hemming glanced at the clock. Half her mind reached out instinctively towards what might be going on in the kitchen and the dining room. Normally at this time of the evening she would be on duty, watchful, ready for problems, instead of just sitting here. She looked unhappy, incapable of giving her full attention to one thing or the other.

At this juncture Detective-Sergeant Campbell arrived at the reception desk and was duly shown in.

The sergeant was a polite, slow-spoken man. He had met Arthur on several occasions when dealing with thefts from various building sites, and more recently when courteously asking a few questions about the corpse of Walter Blythe.

Today he had come to see Mrs Hemming, but seemed pleased rather than disconcerted by the presence of the Johnsons. Perhaps they, too, could help him.

Crime in Lurgate was usually petty, but Campbell was not a man to be upset by mysteries of greater dimensions.

He wondered if Mrs Hemming could tell him anything of the whereabouts of Mr Peter Blythe.

Mrs Hemming bristled. "What's it got to do with me?"

"He was a resident in this hotel."

"For a time."

"I understand he has disappeared."

"Who says so?"

"Hasn't he, then?"

Arthur said: "Where did you get this information, Sergeant?"

"That young chap from the *Chronicle* was here earlier, hoping for an interview."

"*Him!*" said Mrs Hemming.

"He was informed that Mr Peter Blythe was out and that the time of his return was not known. When he talked to one of the maids . . . "

"Which one?"

"When he talked to one of the maids," said Campbell inexorably, "he learnt that Mr Blythe has in fact been missing for two days. Yet I understand his luggage is still on the premises."

"If a guest wants to go away for a few days, it's not up to me to make a fuss about it."

"This is no ordinary guest, Mrs. Hemming. I think we can say that without contradiction?" Campbell impassively studied each of their faces in turn. "But however unusual the person concerned, and the circumstances involved, is it usual for you to have no idea when a guest will be coming back, when your bill is likely to be paid, and whether to put the luggage in store or leave it where it is?"

Mrs Hemming laced her fingers together in her lap. They tightened. Abruptly she burst out: "He could afford to do just what he wanted to, couldn't he? Mr Johnson seems to have set him up nicely. Very nicely, thank you. He'll be off to buy new luggage, I shouldn't wonder. Flashy stuff — I can just see it. Why should he want to come back here? He's got what he came for."

Campbell turned to Arthur. "You gave this Mr Peter Blythe money, sir?"

"A cheque."

"For how much?"

Arthur hesitated. Nell found that she was holding her breath and watching Mrs Hemming's anguished face.

At last he said: "Twenty thousand pounds."

Mrs Hemming let out a howl of despair.

"He asked for fifty," said Arthur. "I told him I thought that excessive. He agreed to take twenty thousand and go away."

"Blackmail?" said Campbell.

"I wouldn't call it that. No. It was a straightforward request. He felt it was his right."

"And you, sir?"

"I had offered to make restitution. I wanted the matter concluded, I accepted his claim, I paid. I could have said no; I chose to say yes."

"He didn't threaten?" said Campbell wistfully. "No question of extortion?"

"None."

"You think he might come back and ask for more?"

"Just what I said," cried Mrs Hemming.

"He won't get any more," said Arthur flatly. "I've done what I believed right. I don't have to do any more. I told him so. He understood."

"I see. Yes. Does look as though he's whizzed off to splash his money around, doesn't it?"

The telephone rang again. Mrs Hemming reached back automatically for it and dully murmured: "Yes. Where? Oh, I'll be right up."

Martin looked at her enquiringly as she went to the door.

"More rats deserting the sinking ship?"

"Room twenty-two wants me to go up personally." She shook her head. "Window coming in, I shouldn't wonder. Or they want dinner served in the room at no extra charge."

Martin was suddenly on his feet. "Just a minute. Room twenty-two — that's *his* room. Unless you've let it to someone else today?"

"Of course I haven't. His bags are still there — and it's still locked."

"He's back, then." Campbell looked disappointed.

Martin went past his mother, and pushed her gently back into the room.

"Let me do it."

"I want some words with that young man," she said.

"No. Leave it to me."

From where she sat, Nell could see him cross the hall to the foot of the stairs. The door swung open. Mrs Hemming stood irresolute with her hand on the knob.

Detective-Sergeant Campbell rubbed his knuckles uneasily along his chin.

They were fixed in their positions for a timeless moment. Then Mrs Hemming tore herself free. She set off after Martin, stamping up the stairs.

"Well," said Campbell. "Looks very much to me as if . . . "

There was a scream. It was Mrs Hemming's voice, strangled almost out of recognition.

Campbell was a big man but he moved fast. He was halfway up the flight before Arthur and Nell could get out of the room. They reached the top to see him holding Mrs Hemming and trying to shake her into silence.

Up here there were no lights on yet. A tall frosted window at the end of the landing shed a pearly twilight on the carpet and on the doors at either side. One door was open. A dark shape lay crumpled on the floor, blocking the doorway.

"Stairs," Campbell was imploring Mrs Hemming. "Are there any more stairs? Another flight down — another way out?"

She waved speechlessly towards the tall window. Campbell hurried along the landing and turned left, out of sight.

Mrs Hemming went down on her knees. Nell tried to bend down beside her, but was pushed unceremoniously back.

Inside the room were two suitcases, tipped over on their sides. Clothes were spilt out across the floor. The shape huddled across the doorway was Martin's — Martin, his face drained of colour in the uncertain dusk, with a deep, dark stain welling from his side.

11

THE flat had not really existed until now. While the decorating and furnishing had been going on, the two of them had tacitly played a game of 'let's pretend' — making decisions about each room, accepting and rejecting advice from Mrs Johnson and Mrs Hemming, yet somehow not acknowledging that any of this related to anything solid and substantial. Until they got back from their honeymoon and settled into it as their home, the flat was not really there.

Now the fancy had to be abandoned. Brigid tried not to be upset. With Fernrock Hotel condemned and scheduled for demolition as soon as possible, it made sense that Mrs Hemming should move into the spare bedroom of the flat for a few weeks. It was even more reasonable that Martin should go straight there when he came out of hospital. Only a selfish child would go on stubbornly insisting on the makebelieve. But selfish and sentimental as it might be, Brigid couldn't help wishing that the place could have remained untrodden and unoccupied until Martin carried her over the threshold. Now he might not even be able to do that: it would depend on the speed with which his wound healed.

He had been lucky. The knife, driven in so savagely, had been deflected by one of his ribs. He had suffered a considerable loss of blood but no more serious damage. By the end of the week he was fit to be allowed home; and home now was the bedroom that he and Brigid were to have shared when they returned from Malta.

Propped up against the pillows when the doctor had gone, he said:

"Well, that's a relief. Up tomorrow."

"He said you were to take it easy."

"Yes. But there don't seem to be any real worries. No complications. Nothing that fresh air and exercise won't settle."

"Exercise?" said Brigid.

"Like this." He leaned towards her and drew her closer to the bed. He kissed her hand and then pulled her down so that he could kiss her lips.

Mrs Hemming came back from seeing the doctor out of the flat.

"He said you were to take it easy," she said accusingly.

Martin sank back with a rueful grimace. Brigid sat defiantly on the edge of the bed.

"He also said," Martin observed, "that I can get up tomorrow."

"Not by rights you shouldn't. Better off where you are."

"I've got things to do."

"They can wait." Mrs Hemming walked round the bed without once glancing at Brigid. "Nothing that can't wait," she said.

Brigid's mother had arranged flowers in a vase on the bedside table. Mrs Hemming twitched the stems into a new pattern and carried the vase round the bed to the small bookcase on the other side.

Martin grinned at Brigid. She did her best to grin back. This was what she most hated. Mrs Hemming would leave a permanent imprint on the place. Even after she had gone, there would be a fidgety ghost drifting from room to room on its campaign of petty disruption.

Martin said: "Any more news about the old dump?"

"So it's the 'old dump' now, is it?" His mother breathed in and out, hard. "And the news . . . " She paused to give it its full strength. "The news is that . . . they're going to blow it up."

"Phew."

"Blow it up. As though there were a war on, or something. Bang — and that's the end of that."

Her voice was stiff with fury, but tears sparkled in her eyes. Brigid reached out to touch her, ready to make sympathetic noises; but Mrs Hemming jerked away.

Martin said: "Never mind, Mum. I'm sure they know what they're doing. And we're insured."

"They just won't take the trouble, that's all. Easier to have a big bang and get it over with."

"Daddy says it wouldn't be right to risk men's lives on an ordinary demolition job," Brigid tried to explain. "The cliff is in a dreadful state. Once they started bashing away at the walls, the whole lot might go without any warning."

"When do we light the blue touch-paper?" asked Martin.

"Not till the Easter holidays are well and truly over."

"Mustn't frighten the holidaymakers away!" said Mrs Hemming. "The Corporation want to see them back next year. Mustn't disturb them, must we?"

She raised her hands as though expecting to find something in them. Their emptiness was an immediate spur. She went towards the door, off in search of an occupation. On the way she glanced back, once, at the picture which dominated the room — a Polish artist's painting of a group of teasels which Martin had seen in Canterbury, liked, and impulsively bought. Brigid approved his taste: the picture was an integral part of the room.

"Couldn't live with that," said Mrs Hemming. "Oh, well . . . " She shrugged, sighed, and made her exit.

"Oh, well," Martin echoed. He pulled Brigid down and kissed her again. Then he said: "Any more news from the outside world? Something really good, you know — calculated to spread gloom and despondency."

"The police haven't found him yet."

"That's the stuff. More!"

"And Daddy's cheque hasn't been paid in anywhere."

"Waiting till he gets back to his native soil, maybe."

"No trace of him having left the country."

The police had no lead on Martin's assailant. They had no lead on Peter Blythe. It could not be established that the two were one and the same; but Detective-Sergeant Campbell believed neither in coincidences nor in random, motiveless stabbing, and he had discreetly put out a description of Peter Blythe, whom the police hoped might be able to help them in their investigations.

Enquiries at ports and airports produced nothing. Long-range enquiries from Lurgate to Rome and Sicily via somewhat complicated channels did not produce much more. The Sicilian authorities appeared to think that the English were up to something sinister, such as planning an invasion, or at the very least a sly infiltration. They began by making out that they didn't know what the English police were talking about, and then wanted to know why they wanted to know all this anyway. In the end, grudgingly, they confirmed that Peter had lived and worked in Palermo, and lived and worked in Rome, just as Peter himself had said. He was reputed to be a good guide, popular with foreign visitors. He knew some of the not too savoury night spots, but had never quite overstepped the law. He was sharp, but knew how far he could go. How far, they demanded, had he gone?

This was something which nobody in Lurgate knew. Even the handful of people who knew all that had happened since Peter's arrival in the town — and this did not include the police — didn't know all the answers. It looked as though Peter had come back to reclaim his precious particles of identification as the Blythe heir, tossing clothes and everything else aside, and then had attacked Martin. But why? He already had a generous cheque in his pocket. There was no cause for vindictiveness. Even if for some perverse reason he held a grudge against Martin, there was little sense in drawing attention to himself at this stage by attempting murder.

But had it really been Martin he was after? The call from Room twenty-two had asked for Mrs Hemming. Martin had taken it on himself to go up in place of his mother. Would she have been attacked if she had got there first? And again, why?

"I've been lying here," said Martin, "going over and over those few minutes in my mind. It's still a blur. I can't get it straight. The light wasn't so good when I went in — you remember what a dismal sky we had? — and I didn't know what hit me. Someone came at me fast, and it was just like being thumped in the side. Not hard — just enough to knock me off balance. I didn't see anything, just felt it. Then it hurt like hell and the whole place went round and round and up and down, and I don't remember a thing after that."

"If he's still around . . . waiting for you to come out . . . "

"Lurking? I can't imagine why."

"But we can't imagine why . . . well, why *any* of it."

Martin hoisted himself into a more comfortable position. He said: "One thing . . . You're not sorry he's gone, are you?"

"Sorry? If only I could be absolutely sure he was right out of the way and we'd never see him again!"

"Good."

"Why? What were you thinking? Martin . . . "

"It just occurred to me that you might have found him interesting. He did have a sort of — well, a kind of sparkle."

"Yes," said Brigid: "like rotten mackerel."

Faintly they heard the telephone ringing. Brigid slid off the bed, but before she could cross the room the receiver was taken from its hook and they heard the murmur of Mrs Hemming's voice.

"Now what?" said Martin.

A minute later his mother came in. This time she looked straight at Brigid. "Your mother phoned to ask if you were here."

"Oh. I'll have a word with her . . . "

"It's all right. She's rung off. She didn't have any special message. Just wanted to tell you not to make a nuisance of yourself."

"To me?" said Martin.

"I think she meant me."

"Am I being a nuisance?" asked Brigid.

"I didn't say you were. Nothing to do with me. After all" — Mrs Hemming looked round the room, her lips pursed — "it's not *my* house, is it?"

She went out again.

Martin began to laugh weakly, then pressed a hand to his side. "Your mother and mine!"

"Do you think we'll ever be able to manage them?"

"Fighting every inch of the way."

"Do you think perhaps they're right?"

"I'm doubtful they could be right about anything — individually or collectively."

"I meant," said Brigid, "about postponing the wedding."

"Do *you* think so?"

"Darling, you know I don't want to . . . "

"You're afraid I'll be too feeble to satisfy you?"

She felt herself reddening. "No. I don't get that impression at all."

"You're worried about being tied to a potential invalid all your life?"

"Martin, don't talk rubbish."

"Then don't talk rubbish. You're going to marry me — date and time as scheduled. Right?"

"Right," said Brigid.

In spite of all the lunatic upheavals of recent weeks it was impossible not to feel happy.

A sprinkling of holidaymakers joined the throng outside the church. It was an extra treat for the women visitors. They cooed sentimentally as the bride emerged from the shadows of the porch.

Martin pressed her arm against his side.

Familiar faces turned upwards, some friendly and some merely curious. Among the locals there were plently who had come simply to stare, to accuse someone, somewhere, of somehow hushing something up. It was as though the wedding itself might just possibly be a conspiracy.

"Wouldn't be surprised if they hadn't

215

done that other one in as well. Not a sight or sound of him . . . "

Brigid had not been a devout church-goer, but standing at the top of the steps she sensed the weight of it, and at the same time the gracefulness of it, behind her. It had been a part of her life for so long. With a sharpened physical awareness of everything today — the smell and sound and feel of things; the sight of the finely chiselled stone face of Sir Richard Welling, benefactor of this parish, beaming blankly yet reassuringly down at her during the ceremony; the ageless chill of the nave and the warmth of old Mr Hadow's voice — she was acutely conscious of being alive. She tasted the savours of Lurgate on her tongue as she looked out over the sea: tang of salt and of woodsmoke, sweetness of the flowerbeds along the promenade and the blossom she was carrying; and the faint, acrid, dusty smell of the road, and the metallic warmth of the waiting car.

Martin was beside her, close to her. They went down the steps to the car.

The reception was to have been held in Fernrock. Now it had been switched to the Copperfield Hotel, obscurely so named because, according to a plaque in the dining room, Charles Dickens had stayed here while writing a few chapters of *Barnaby Rudge*.

Mrs Hemming paced round the tables. She examined the tablecloths for stains and the wedding cake for cracks in the icing. "If only we'd been able to have it where we *ought* to have had it . . . " She circled round a large spray of flowers, and sniffed.

Mrs Johnson talked gaily and a trifle shrilly to her friends and Brigid's friends. Then she detached herself from one chattering group and joined Mrs Hemming, taking her arm and walking round the room with her. They were both tense and both terribly affable. Brigid got the impression that from the corners of their fixed smiles they were contriving to carry on an argument about trivialities of which even thirty seconds later they would deny all knowledge.

Brigid's father winked at her.

"Always the same. Families. Part of the ritual — bristling at each other. It was much worse at our own wedding, though

I don't imagine your mother lets herself remember it."

A self-conscious line of people waited to shake hands with the bride and groom. It all seemed a bit solemn. Sarah Iggulden spoilt it by giggling when she reached Brigid. It was certainly a bit odd to be going through this formality with a girl you'd known for fifteen years and with whom you hadn't once in your life shaken hands until now.

At last they began to split up and form new groups round the buffet tables. Brigid felt dizzy. She clung to Martin's hand, and he steadied her.

"Malta, you're going to?" A girl called Veronica, with a twentyish fringe and a hat of pink petals, looked wisely over her champagne glass. "Of course you'll take some of your foreign currency allowance as well? I mean, it's so easy to hop over to Tunis or somewhere. Pity to miss it while you're in the Med." She had spent two holidays on Ibiza, and knew all the places one could hop to.

The speeches were short and not too embarrassing. The ritual was not so awful as Brigid had feared. A few of the girls were growing as arch and sniggery as Sarah, but the people around kept them subdued.

I want to be out of here, thought Brigid. The pressure of voices, even the rational and amiable onces, grew too intense. I want to be with Martin — that's what all this is *for*, but what on earth has it really got to do with it?

Her mother came up beside her and kissed her. It was a warm, instinctive kiss. Brigid wanted to hug her; but she did wish her mother did not have to look so ruefully defeated when she glanced at Martin.

Again her father winked.

The groups reshuffled. Mrs Hemming was talking with beligerent matiness to an elderly woman in a corner; the Johnsons split up and made brief, dutiful forays into the different clusters of guests; Martin's best man came towards Martin and stood without saying a word for a minute or more. He was a colleague from the research centre, devoted to his work and shy with anyone who did not understand his professional language.

"Not going too badly," he managed at last.

It was a noble effort at general conversation.

"Let me top up your glass," said Martin.

"No, this is plenty, thanks. Plenty."

Brigid said: "Thank you for keeping your speech so neat and short, Eric."

He flushed and said, "Oh," and, "Well, you know . . . short and sour, that's me." He laughed. They all laughed. Martin slapped him lightly and affectionately on the back. Brigid could never be at ease with Eric the way Martin was, but she liked him, and wasn't sure that she didn't in fact envy him: it must be wonderful to have such a passion for one's work — a vocation, in Eric's case.

"I've told them," squealed Veronica from the far side of the room, "that they simply must hop over to Lampedusa. Such a waste not to, when you're in that part of the world. Sicily, of course, has been spoilt. Overdone . . . "

"So you haven't given any more thought to the Ryneside project?" Eric was saying.

"Enough on my mind," Martin replied in a voice so muted that Brigid only just caught the words.

"You're the obvious candidate."

"Me and a hundred others."

"No. You." Eric sounded unusually fervent. On his own subject he was a man transformed. "It fits in with all that work you've been doing on acaricides. A new application like this . . . the facilities you'd be given for broadening the basis of research . . . "

"You're very anxious to get rid of me, aren't you?"

Brigid said: "What on earth are you two talking about?"

Eric stared as though at a complete stranger, then said: "Hasn't he told you?"

"Told me what?"

"This new international project they're setting up on . . . "

"This," said Martin with a flamboyant gesture which was too showy to be convincing, "is my wedding day. Can we save the shop talk?"

"Sorry."

Brigid said: "I'd still like to know . . . "

"We're not quite ready to move," Martin

said to Eric. "Not yet. We'd like to have a housewarming party in our nice new flat before we decide to leave it. It could be, old son, that we'll be *happy* there. Any objections?"

"And who's talking of moving?" demanded Brigid.

"Nobody. The paint's not dry yet."

Mrs Hemming must have been close enough to hear a large part of this. "It's all right." She set herself firmly before her son and Brigid. "I don't want you to worry. You're not to let yourselves fret while you're away."

"Mum, nobody's going to fret."

"I'll be out of there before you get back. I don't want you to think I'll be round your necks the whole time. It wouldn't be fair. It's not right for a young couple . . . "

Brigid's father appeared suddenly and steered Mrs Hemming away. He gave her another glass of champagne.

Brigid was about to turn back to Martin and ask what on earth they had been talking about, insisting on getting a straight answer, when she noticed a heavy, broad-shouldered man come into the room. He was too large to be unobtrusive, but he was doing his best to be tactful.

It was Detective-Sergeant Campbell. He trod slowly round the room, looking quietly preoccupied, like a detective hired to keep a discreet eye on the wedding presents. Without drawing attention to his presence he edged behind three women and reached Brigid's father.

He spoke. It could have been only a few words, but they were enough to make Mr Johnson go pale.

Brigid instinctively began to hurry across the room towards her father. From another corner, moving in at a tangent, came her mother.

The body of Peter Blythe had been found.

He could not quite be called the skeleton at the feast, since there was still flesh on his bones; but that flesh, Campbell intimated, had suffered from being immersed in sea-water and rasped against the iron, barnacle-encrusted girders of the pier.

12

"LODGED in the girders," said Campbell quietly, "below high water mark. The speedboats haven't been running this last week because of the weather, or the body would have been spotted sooner. It was only a few yards from the pleasure trip landing-stage."

"Accident?" said Arthur.

"Could be."

But Nell found little comfort in Campbell's answer. He conceded the possibility; but she sensed that he was not readily going to accept it.

She said: "He could have fallen over?"

"Might have done. But there's a pretty secure rail there. You'd have to try hard to chuck yourself off. And he wasn't a kid — not the sort who'd be skylarking about and climbing all over the place."

Martin crossed the room and joined Brigid. Nell glanced up at the clock above the door of the room. The two of them would soon have to go and change if they were to leave on time.

"He could have been pushed," said Campbell. "Or knocked out and dragged down the steps to the speedboat platform."

"Are you accusing anyone?" asked Arthur.

"Not yet."

"Weren't there any witnesses?"

"It's holiday time," Nell added. "There must have been people about."

"It's been mighty blowy out on the end there. Late in the evenings there aren't many who'd want to go out on the pier. Plenty of opportunity for rough stuff once it got dark."

"If people wouldn't want to go along there, why should *he* have gone? He . . . he comes from a southern climate" — Nell knew she was talking too much, and at random, but could not stop herself — "and he'd be the last one to go out gulping in great mouthfuls of an English gale."

Detective-Sergeant Campbell shrugged. "We don't know. Don't see how we can know, right now. We'll have to question people, that's all. A lot of people." He stared dourly into the arduous future.

"There's a lot of questioning we'll have to get down to."

"Starting right here?" said Arthur.

The two men weighed each other up. Neither smiled, and neither looked away.

Nell said: "Look, Brigid and Martin have to go. They've got a train and a plane to catch. You don't need them hanging about here, do you?"

"It struck me," said Campbell deliberately, "that with a wedding on, they might be dashing off. I just wanted to make sure it wasn't one of these secret honeymoon addresses — lost to the world, that sort of thing."

"You don't think they had anything to do with . . . well, this awful business?"

"I'm not allowing myself to think anything yet. But Peter Blythe was a bit of a nuisance to your family, I'd say, and you're the only ones in Lurgate who know much about him."

"Precious little."

"You've had more to do with him than anyone else. You're the only ones with any reason for . . . "

"For what?" snapped Arthur.

"For any disagreement. Sorry, Mr

Johnson, but I do have to find out, you know. It's my job. And I do have to check where all the family is — and where it's going to be."

"Malta," said Martin tersely. "That's where we shall be. Nothing secret about it. I can give you the name of the hotel."

Campbell looked dubious. "Going abroad?"

"Not exactly abroad." Arthur's temper was fraying. Nell knew the symptoms. It was only at such times that he was liable to grow sarcastic. "It's in the sterling area. George Cross, bags of British loyalty and all that. A sort of Mediterranean Isle of Wight — can't we count it as home waters?"

The detective allowed his gaze to wander slowly over the guests. Already heads were turning. Mrs Hemming showed signs of coming over, then swung round and presented the group with a view of her back. She dissociated herself from any further scandals and horrors. She had had enough.

"There's no reason," said Nell, "why they shouldn't be allowed to leave now — is there?"

227

"Well . . . "

"If there is, say quite clearly what it is," said Arthur.

"We haven't got that far yet. You know that, sir. I just came round to tell you the news . . . "

"And to see how we took it? All right, you've seen. Now these youngsters are going to change and get out of here."

Brigid glanced at Martin. He nodded almost imperceptibly. Nell felt a sad twinge of jealousy. All at once Brigid had moved a long, long way from her. Already, she thought: already Brigid and Martin were close enough to communicate without words, to understand and share and react as one person — a person made up from the two of them.

So soon. So irrevocably.

Brigid said: "Daddy, we can't leave now. If anything crops up . . . "

"Go and change, my dear." Arthur put his arm round her shoulders and kissed her cheek. "You'll have to get a move on if you're going to catch that train."

"But with all this going on . . . "

"Do as your father tells you," said Nell.

"Wait a minute." Martin smiled, but his left elbow jutted forward a few inches as though to take the brunt of an attack. "I'm the boss now."

"Oh." Upset as she was, Brigid could not help answering his smile. "Out of the frying-pan . . . ?"

"All right," said Nell. "What do *you* think she should do?"

"Just what her father says. Get a move on and come away with me. Now!"

"But leave that hotel address," said Detective-Sergeant Campbell.

There was a lull. Nell, tingling with a hot irritation like a couple of viruses fighting something out in her bloodstream, thought that Campbell could at least have gone away for half an hour and come back later. But he simply stood politely to one side and pretended not to watch. He managed to be both discreet and monstrously obtrusive.

When Brigid and Martin reappeared, it was all over too quickly. Nell did not want a big emotional scene, but somehow she had expected the tempo of the farewells to be more leisurely. She wanted to hold Brigid back just for a few minutes longer;

wanted there to be a slow, gentle parting rather than a brutal snap. The noise and laughter welled up, Brigid threw a sprig of blossom to someone, Mrs Hemming burst into tears, all the occupants of the room surged towards the door as though at a signal, as though a fire alarm had begun its clamour in all their heads.

"Goodbye, Mummy. Bless you."

And it was over. Martin kissing her, Brigid hugging her father, everyone shouting silly, meaningless things. And they were gone, almost thrown out.

Guests began to leave. Nell shook hands with three young men who might or might not have been friends of Martin. Others smiled and waved, a couple of women dabbed at their eyes and said it had been wonderful. The room was emptying. Two girls came in and started to clear away the litter from the table. There was a percussive clatter as plates were stacked and removed.

Mrs Hemming decided to join forces with the Johnsons after all. She oozed hostility towards Campbell.

Again doubts stirred within Nell, stronger this time. Now there was a corpse to add to the insoluble equation, and this meant that there must also be a killer. Whatever she might say to Campbell, Nell did not really believe in an accident.

Betty Hemming . . . or Arthur?

It could not possibly be Arthur. She would have known. He couldn't have kept it from her.

Mrs Hemming said: "Something's happened, hasn't it?"

Campbell raised an eyebrow. Nell was tempted to tell him the whole story of Mrs Hemming and her ancestry. Let him see, then, who had the strongest motive for murder.

Arthur said: "I think Mrs Hemming ought to know the full story — remember what happened to Martin. It must all tie in somehow." As Campbell hesitated, he said: "A glass of champagne, Sergeant?"

Campbell accepted a drink and, for the second time, told briefly of the discovery under the pier.

Mrs Hemming's face seemed to shrivel in on itself. She might have been in acute pain. "Is it going to go on like this?" she whispered. "On . . . and on?"

Then the lines softened and she gave a harsh, abrupt laugh. "No. Of course not. That . . . that creature's dead, you say? So that settles it."

"Not quite," said Campbell softly. "We still want to know who killed him — if anyone *was* involved."

"He was drunk." Mrs Hemming's confident contempt was grotesque. "All that money . . . I told you it'd be squandered. Drank himself into a stupor — fell in the water. Just what I'd have expected."

"Charming, Mrs Johnson." Mr Hadow bobbed up suddenly before them. "Such a delightful couple. A delightful afternoon." He shook hands with Nell and then with Mrs Hemming. He was so mild and twinkling and benevolent that he threatened to topple over into a carricature of himself. "It must be a great joy for you ladies. And you, Mr Johnson."

The two ladies made suitable noises, Arthur walked to the door with the vicar, and Campbell took a leisurely sip at his drink, waiting for Arthur to return.

Nell said: "How long was he . . . it . . . under the pier?"

Arthur came back within range, and Campbell said: "A week . . . ten days. Difficult to establish within a few days because of the — um — state of the body. Taken a bit of a battering, like I told you."

"So he could have been dead the evening Martin was attacked. Or alive, which would mean he could have been the attacker."

"Dead — or alive," Campbell agreed. "Neater if he was alive. But it still don't tell us how *he* finished up the way he did."

"Accident," said Nell.

"Drunk," said Mrs Hemming. "Serve him right."

Campbell studied the two women in turn, and then raised an enquiring eyebrow at Arthur. Arthur did not speak.

Nell burst out: "I know what it'll be like. There'll be a nice little story going round the town. My husband's following in his father's footsteps — that's it, isn't it? Killing a Blythe — pushing Walter Blythe's grandson off the pier."

"No accounting for what people will say," said Campbell smoothly.

"More hints and nudges. And no chance of answering back."

Arthur answered Campbell's steady gaze. "Why should I have had anything to do with it, Sergeant?"

"I'm not saying you did, sir."

"Not in so many words. But theoretically, if I really were involved — what motive? Any ideas?"

"You might have wanted to stop him cashing the cheque."

"I could have stopped it at the bank."

"Then he'd just have come back for more, wouldn't he? No point in giving it him in the first place, sir, if you weren't going to let him cash it. Unless . . ."

"All right, all right." Arthur brusquely accepted this.

"The cheque!" cried Nell. "Was it on the body?"

"No."

"And the key of his room?" asked Mrs Hemming.

"No key, either. We carried out a thorough examination. His pockets were in a bit of a mess — all waterlogged. But no cheque and no key. Could be at the bottom of the sea, of course."

At the inquest on Peter Blythe an open verdict was returned.

"Another case of 'not proven'," said Nell bitterly.

The cloud was darker than the one which had hung over them after the discovery of Walter Blythe's corpse. It was heavier and closer and would take a long time to blow away.

Arthur had been called to give evidence regarding the arrival of Peter Blythe in Lurgate and his own contacts with the young man up to the time of his disappearance. He was not himself on trial; but where there was no charge, there could be no acquittal.

In silence they drove home. It was not until he turned off the ridge that Arthur, glancing back over the roofs of the town, said:

"It'd be good to get out of here. Turn our backs on the blasted place once and for all."

"Is that what you want?"

"There are some big scheme brewing up North. The centre of gravity in this country is shifting, and about time, too. They've got some real projects up there.

Real. Jobs you could get your teeth into."

He was driving steadily but seemed not to be watching the road. He saw something far ahead, a long way off; saw a challenge he wanted to accept. Something he could get his teeth into, thought Nell. He had been loyal and conscientious too long. She said levelly:

"Darling, if you want us to go, there's no reason why we shouldn't. We'll only be suffocated if we stay here."

He drove up to their garage and leaned across Nell to open her door for her. She got out. When he had put the car away he came slowly, ruminatively into the house.

"It'd be too much like running away," he said. "I'm afraid I'll have to stick it out. We'll leave when the whole thing is cleared up."

"If it ever is. Think of old Blythe — or his widow, Serafina or whatever she was called. *She* didn't stay. She must have got tired of being goggled at, jeered at, suspected of God knows what. She upped and cleared out. Why not us?"

"Do you suppose she was easy in her mind, afterwards?"

"That's something we can't even guess at."

"Peter wasn't very informative about that aspect, but I did get the impression that she harboured a lot of bitterness."

"We can't know," Nell insisted. "And it wouldn't be the same for us, anyway. There's the two of us. If you want to go, we go. No regrets. Never mind what the rest of them say."

"You're wonderful," he said shakily.

They sat down together and he put his arm round her. She rested her head on his shoulder. In spite of the turmoil he had suffered since this wretched business began she was still conscious of his basic, unshakable strength. He was still the staunch one; still loving and protective. She was the one who ought to be giving support and reassurance, but selfishly she was content just to lie against him and close her eyes.

"I hope Brigid's happy," she said. "I hope it works for her, all of it, as marvellously as it's always worked for me."

"For us," he said. The strain and the worry had gone from his voice.

13

THE sun through the slatted shutters cast a dappled pattern on Martin's shoulder. Brigid kissed the warmth of it. He rolled lazily yet purposefully towards her.

"We ought to get up, I suppose." She yawned contentedly. "The sun's shining."

"It'll keep shining. The travel brochures guaranteed that. We'll demand our money back if there's any slackness."

His hand wandered possessively over her. When they talked, they found themselves often not finishing the sentences. Their hands explored greedily and lovingly, saying more than words could have expressed.

"Perhaps this afternoon . . . "

"Never mind the afternoon. We haven't used up the morning yet. My love . . . "

"So warm . . . "

"Come here. Come on, come here when I tell you."

Martin made love as though revenging

himself for all the frustrations, the waiting, the upsets of the last few weeks. But it was a loving revenge; and with it he showed also a tenderness which made her feel shielded, safe, sheltered.

Brigid said: "When we get back . . . "

"Don't talk about getting back. We're here!"

But by the third day they found themselves, inevitably, talking about Peter Blythe and Brigid's parents and Mrs Hemming. They ought to be talking about their own future, but that couldn't exist until the past had been tidied up.

"Your mother never gave you any idea about . . . well, about your grandfather: Not until that day when it all came out?"

"Not a word. And it still means nothing to me. I don't feel like Walter Blythe's grandson. I feel like me."

"Yes," she said, touching him. "You do. Tell me when you feel like *me*."

"Right now."

They dismissed thoughts of Lurgate and all the questions that couldn't be answered; but infuriatingly the questions kept coming back.

Brigid tried to talk about the two of them only. About themselves, apart from the others who crowded in on them. Detached, separate, self-sufficient.

"What was all that, at the wedding, about another job for you?"

"Oh, that. It'd mean us moving out — going up to Newcastle."

"That's the only thing against it?"

"I'm not ready for it anyway. Too much of a gamble."

"What *is* the job?" she asked.

Martin explained reluctantly, as though unwilling to let himself dwell on the idea for too long. "It's a kind of preproduction parasite control. Stop pests before they start. Nothing essentially new in it, but this time they're planning an international consortium. That's one snag: get a lot of nations together, and they'll be playing politics instead of getting on with the job."

"But the job?" she insisted. "The job in itself?"

"Ideally it should cover all exports from Western Europe to developing countries. Research on pest problems at this end, and control of material when it gets to the other. At its simplest, imagine a big export consignment of wood proofed against parasites. All done according to a sort of European Standards Specification. Pestproofed exports — and aftersales service on problems arising in individual countries or with individual customers. Cut down waste, destruction . . . and a large amount of human illness, under proper control. At the same time it would have to be done without disturbing the ecological balance."

"Sounds fascinating."

"It could be."

"You'd better tell me a lot more about it, so I'll know what to think."

"Now?"

"Well . . . "

Their bodies were together again, and she forgot about his job and the future and the past and their parents and about all problems other than the one of how best to prolong this ecstasy.

They loved and they lazed. They wandered through the streets of Valletta, some of the walls dazzling white and cream, others peeling and crumbling before their eyes. There was the clip-clop of horses drawing the karozzins, the muted music in some restaurants and the blare of it in a discothèque. They joined a party on a motor cruiser exploring the bays, but jibbed at the idea of water-skiing. "Too energetic," sighed Brigid. And they laughed, and loved again.

One day Brigid went shopping for a few trinkets. It was the first time she had been on her own. She felt frightened not so much of her surroundings or the people in the streets as of this awareness of her dependence on Martin. It was appalling. She laughed to herself and found she was hoping that it would always be the same.

She studied a poster in a travel agency window, with a timetable in small print lying below it. When she got back to their hotel she said:

"Did you know it's possible to fly over to Sicily from here? To Palermo."

"Yes, I know."

"You mean you've checked, too?"

"Yes."

"Why?"

"Curiosity."

"If we're both that curious . . . "

"We ought to go a bit further."

"Just out of curiosity. I mean, we couldn't hope to learn anything really important. But Veronica was right: it's silly to be here and not hop over somewhere."

"I've been to the bank," said Martin. "I've got the currency we'll need."

"Already? You'd already decided?"

"Yes."

"It's . . . settled, then. We do have to go."

"I think we do."

Seen from above as they banked to run in, the line of the coast was a parched brown shadow on the steely blue sheen of the sea. When they landed, it was to find that the crags and splintered teeth of the hills had receded, leaving a narrow strip of level country by the sea. They were driven into Palermo through a scattering of dusty houses, a tangle of suburbs, and sudden bright boulevards.

Tall houses leaned out over the streets. Washing flapped like banners from the tiers of iron balconies.

Martin had booked in advance for two

nights. They found themselves in a third-rate hotel, the others being full. They didn't know how long they would be staying. Brigid's first impulse was to turn and flee: the place was dazzling, dirty, colourful and utterly alien. She resolved not to be fanciful, but could not shrug off a sensation of lowering menace — this was, and felt like, a land of earthquakes and volcanic temperaments.

The men eyed her as she went into the hotel. They eyed her when she and Martin sat outside a café. Small, dark and virile, they leaned against walls, propped their elbows on tables, and studied her. They were unsettling without ever being offensive. It was a nakedly sexual curiosity, without slyness. A dozen times she seemed to see Peter's eyes again — greedy, appreciative, yet half-mocking.

Martin spotted the tourist bureau first. It was closed and would not be open until the next morning. Here, if anywhere, they would know Peter Blythe, who had been a guide in Palermo before going to Rome. There was also the headquarters of the carabinieri . . . but somehow they were reluctant to march in there and ask awkward questions. It was a relief, in a way, that the tourist bureau was shut: it provided an excuse for waiting until tomorrow.

They spent the evening eating, drinking, and sauntering. Small streets led down to the water, crowded with stalls and garish with naked electric light bulbs. The gutters were clogged with refuse. There was colour, and in the alleys there was darkness; there were smells and noise, and there were cars honking and blaring and nudging their way through the drifting crowds. There was no focus, no general pattern — just a swirl and shuffle of movement and noise.

They made love that night in a room with a sagging ceiling and flaky walls. There was a faint, all-permeating smell of sweat and cooking. A fight broke out in the street below their window, and in the small hours of the morning somebody somewhat began to wail a sad, interminable song.

In the morning they went to the tourist bureau as soon as it was open.

The manager was an incongruously tall

245

man with a long, sallow face and very long fingers, the joints tufted with wispy black hair. At the first few words of English he began affably to produce brochures from under the counter.

Martin said: "We were wondering . . . did you ever know Peter Blythe? Or Pietro, I suppose he'd have been called here."

The manager tapped the counter with a sheaf of leaflets he was holding. "You come from . . . from where?"

"From England. We'd like to talk to anyone who knew him."

"Already I answer the questions from Roma. The police — I have told them all I know. And still I do not know why. He is in trouble? He has the troubles with the English police?"

"Not any more," said Martin cryptically.

"He showed you round the island once before, maybe? Or you know him in Roma? Yes?"

"No."

The manager shrugged. "Please, I do not know what you want. He is a guide, we know him, he works good. But nothing to do with me."

"He lived locally?"

"Outside Palermo," said the man, just as Peter himself had said it. "Inland. He comes from Manciano."

"How does one get to Manciano?"

"But it is not a place to go. Is nothing, Manciano. Look, I show you — we have a tour starting an hour from now. Our beautiful places ... historic ruins ... earthquake devastation now, also. Nothing to do in Manciano. You take a trip in our coach, you see better Sicily than that."

"We'd like to go," said Martin, "just to have a look round."

"The trip, yes?"

"Manciano," said Martin.

Brigid slipped her arm through his. She felt that he was liable to start marching across the island any moment on his own two feet, and she wanted to be sure he didn't leave her behind.

The manager sighed and said: "The tour bus goes across the island. At an angle, so." He half turned and drew a sketchy line with his finger across the yellowing map on the wall. "You can get off at Prizzi — here. Then it is down the road . . . not a good road, I am warning you . . . on the way to Calascibetta."

"Could we hire a taxi?" asked Brigid.

His smile grew patronising. "There is a man with a car."

"We could telephone ahead . . . "

"The coach," he said. "Sometimes it starts a little late, you know. Or there are difficulties on the road. I would be wrong, I must not tell you a time it arrives at Prizzi. Far better you go on the whole tour and come back safely, I think."

Martin looked at Brigid. She squeezed his arm.

He said: "We'll get off at Prizzi."

The coach was half empty. An American couple sat hunched in one of the front seats, and at the back were three elderly Germans. The other travellers appeared improbably to be peasants from the interior, using the coach as a convenient way of getting back from a brisk shopping expedition in Palermo.

Brigid settled herself by the window and stared out.

They bumbled across a stretch of well-cultivated land, rich with orange and lemon groves, and on through flanking acres of artichoke and potato crops. Then the coach began to climb, coughing and grumbling as it did so. It slowed through a tumbledown village where flocks of sheep and goats appeared to be having a convention.

The hills grew steeper. On the farther slopes the sheep were like clots of dingy snow among the humped grey boulders.

An hour went by. The sun struck in viciously, first on Brigid's neck and then against her cheek. Her eyes were tired but she had to watch, had to see and store up everything that passed.

At Prizzi the driver argued with them, obviously imploring them to continue on his gay sight-seeing tour. They got down and watched the bus clatter away in a cloud of grit.

There was no car; no car that could be found by two diffident English people, anyway.

They began to walk down the road. They had covered a hot, dusty mile or so when a donkey plodded up behind them, drawing a flamboyantly painted cart. Its driver was dark, small and withdrawn.

His sombre face clashed absurdly with the gaiety of his cart. He said a few words, recognised their uselessness, and jerked his thumb to indicate that Brigid should ride in the cart. He made room for her, then slid down and walked stolidly beside Martin.

Thirty minutes later they reached Manciano.

It had been visible from some distance away. From a ragged hummock of land it peered out suspiciously over the eye-aching rise and fall of the land. On one shoulder a crumbling palace's whiteness collapsed into brown streaks and a tangle of parched grass. The road curled and wound up to it along a spine of rock, flanked by cypresses.

The balconies here were the shabbiest replicas of those in Palermo. There was no colour other than the hazed white and brown, providing a backdrop for men and women in black — the women in black shawls and lustreless dark dresses, many of the men in hooded capes like those of an austere religious order.

Here, also, the men's heads turned. They were slow and sullently hostile rather than greedy: a woman like Brigid, they implied in every dragged-out movement, ought not to exist.

Martin and Brigid crossed the piazza, at a loss. They had no idea where to go, whom to approach.

Outside a bar men leaned against the wall and muttered. If they were arguing, there was no fervour in it. One younger man stood apart from the main group, twisting his hands obsessively in the sunlight.

Brigid said: "I'm glad you're with me."

"I'm glad I'm with you, too. It's habit-forming."

"You don't think something awful will happen?"

"My main worry is that nothing at all will happen. None of them look very communicative. But we're here now, and we're not going back empty-handed."

They went on, casually studying the decrepit façades as though they were trippers who could be relied on to stroll out of the far end of the town and not reappear.

Suddenly a priest crossed the piazza,

scurrying along at a speed which did not seem natural in this slumberous town of this corner of the island, Martin called out, but the priest vanished like a dark, persecuted animal into a doorway.

They found themselves in front of a shop, the only obvious one in the square. Its window sported a few cigar packets faded by the sun, some unidentifiable bottles, a few magazines, and a row of picture postcards which even in their prime could hardly have been the most enticing propaganda for the district.

Martin led Brigid towards the door. "Let's start here."

They went in.

The interior of the shop was stuffy, clogged with darkness after the harsh glare of the piazza. For some long seconds there was no response to the squawk of the opening door and Martin's rap on the counter. Then a middle-aged man stooped through the low door at the back of the shop.

Martin spoke very slowly. "I wonder if you can tell us anything about the Blythes? They used to live here."

The man put his head on one side,

mumbled an inaudible question, and hopefully picked up a folder of black-and-white photographs.

"The Blythes," said Martin again. He managed to sound neither pessimistic nor aggressive. Patiently he said: "They lived here in Manciano. There would have been Serafina in the old days . . . and not long ago Peter, or Pietro . . . "

They might just as well set about finding their way back to Palermo, thought Brigid. The sooner the better.

The man turned and called through the open door into the room from which he had emerged. A girl's voice answered. He stood aside to let her come out and take his place at the counter.

She was about twenty, with raven-black hair trailing sleekly down over her shoulders. Her eyes had a deep golden tobacco glow.

"I help you, please?"

She was not beautiful but there was a captivating eagerness in her face. To Brigid the lilt of her voice was pure music. They had been madly optimistic and arrogant, expecting to find anyone here who could or would speak English;

but they were in luck.

Joyfully Martin said: "You speak English!"

"I learn. A little, you know. I go to the town to learn. You wish to buy souvenir?"

"Well, er . . . "

The father was watching. Brigid nudged Martin, but it was unnecessary: he was already taking money from his pocket. Free information had to be paid for, whether they wanted picture postcards or not.

The father made a wet, unintelligible noise with his lips. His attention did not wander for a second.

"A couple of postcards, I think," said Martin.

The girl spread out six tolerably new cards over the display of magazines. As Martin was about to select one, her father groped under the counter and produced a book. He laid it proudly over one of the cards.

It was a book about the island of Sicily and its customs, and it was written in English. From its appearance, one would assume it had been published in the nineteen-thirties and had lain here, coated with a camouflage of dust, during and after the war years. The cover had warped, and the tops of the pages were almost sepia by now.

The girl looked embarrassed and said something in an undertone to her father. He straightened up and tapped the book with his forefinger as though to give a personal testimonial to its quality.

"We'll buy it," said Martin.

Half-ashamed, the girl handed it over to him and took coins from his outstretched palm. When she stopped, her father gave an agitated cough and snarled something at her. She snarled back. He turned away.

"And now," said Martin, "I wonder if you can tell us anything about the Blythes?"

The girl glanced swiftly at her father, then lifted a creaking flap and came round the counter.

"Pietro?" she said. "He is in trouble?"

"Everybody always expects Pietro to be in trouble," Martin commented.

Brigid tried to decide from the girl's face whether she knew a lot of secrets or was merely anxious to give them their money's worth.

She said: "Did you know them at all well?"

"In Manciano, we all know. Everything, it is known. So, the disgrace, you know. When there is the news, then so much laughter."

"The news?"

"About the grand *signora*. She is a widow, yes, but not the . . . I am sorry, it is not easy for me . . . not the widow like she tells us. It is not true, so much."

"The *signora*?" Brigid was baffled.

"Then comes Pietro. Always if there is bad news, it is Pietro brings it. Always if things are bad, somehow they are good for Pietro."

The girl spoke rapidly to her father and then led the way to the outer door. She stepped out into the sunlight, motioning Brigid and Martin to follow. They crossed a square of hot brightness and then went along a narrow alley. At the end was a smaller open space, less grand than the piazza but more graceful. One side of it was taken up entirely by the wall and ornamental railing of a single house. The house itself, almost a tiny *palazzo*, stood back behind a flagged courtyard. Through a gateway they could glimpse another, interior courtyard, almost Spanish in style. The building and its surroundings were in good condition, standing out from the rest of the little town with aristocratic disdain.

"Now it is all Manciano who laughs," said the girl. Abruptly she swung round upon Brigid, and this time the eagerness in her face was almost pathetic. "You think there is work for me in England? I come away, I work, I am not in Manciano any more. You think?"

"Well, I don't know. I mean, it would depend on what you want to do." Brigid could hardly bear the intensity of that yearning gaze.

"I go anywhere, I do anything."

Martin said firmly: "This was the Blythe house?"

"Yes."

The finely wrought balcony and the shutters had all been painted more recently than anything else in the neighbouring streets.

Brigid said: "It doesn't look as though

Serafina and the rest of them were quite as humble as Peter made out. Or did we misinterpret him?"

"If there was a phoney way of telling a thing, you may be sure . . . "

"Please?" The girl looked from one to the other, hating to miss the slightest addition to her knowledge of the language.

Martin said: "Mrs Blythe lived here? Mrs Serafina Blythe?"

"Is so, yes. Since I am a little girl, and before that, yes."

"When did she die?"

"Die?" The girl's hand flew to her mouth. "She is dead?"

"Well . . . isn't she?"

Her hand strayed down her chin. She raised her shoulders, puzzled, leaning imploringly towards them as though once more she might have missed some fine nuance of English speech. Carefully, to make sure that they were all talking about the same thing, she said:

"She was not dead two, three weeks ago. She was alive when she left here."

14

ONE wall of Fernrock had developed an ominous split during the night. It zigzagged down the brickwork, pouring out a fine dust down the slope. Cracks were already splaying across many of the windows some because of the gentle shifting and settling of the building, some because children had seized the opportunity of throwing stones. "Trippers," said Mrs Hemming fiercely. "Kids from London — not the sort of folk who belong in Lurgate at all."

The area was roped off and danger signs erected. It was decided that the fabric was too shaky to be left much longer, and the demolition date was brought forward. A van removed the larger pieces of Mrs Hemming's furniture and took them into store. Nell helped to transfer personal belongings in her car.

"And that's what all that work amounted to. All that work we put into it, all those years." Mrs Hemming looked back over her shoulder as Nell drove away. "Now they can't wait to pull it down."

When it was out of sight behind the trees, she looked to her front again, watching the road as though it might at any moment fill up with a legion of enemies.

Nell said: "It was an awful responsibility, though. When you've got over the shock, I'm sure you'll find things are a lot easier."

"Derelict. After the war, when we took it on, it wasn't much more than a ruin. That's how we got it so cheap. And we worked and slaved on it, and we had something to be proud of. I don't see why I shouldn't say so. Proud of it, we were."

"Yes," said Nell soothingly. "You did a wonderful job."

"And then he has to go and get himself killed in Korea. Ought never to have gone. At his age, there was no need for him to go."

"No," said Nell. She had heard it so often before.

"Though mind you" — the odd spurt of feminine conceit was uncharacteristic

— "he was younger than I was."

They completed the long, wide arc behind the town and drew up outside the block of flats. The communal garden was still rough and unmade, but the paths had been finished off, and already more than half the flats were occupied.

At the door, one arm laden with a motley assortment of her possessions, Mrs Hemming fumbled for her key. Then she let out a clucking gasp of annoyance; her tongue went stuttering on against the roof of her mouth.

"I must have left them behind. My keys! In the hotel."

"I've still got my spare." Nell opened her bag and found the key. She let them in. Mrs Hemming lowered her bits and pieces on to the narrow shelf along the side of the hall.

"I must go back and get them. There's this key, and all the keys for the hotel. I'm not going to have them lying around."

"We'll pick them up on the way back."

They went on into the flat. Nell looked round. The signs of Mrs Hemming's occupation were immediately apparent. It was not just that the place was tidy: it was prim. Nell had been brought up to favour a style of decoration in which nothing was unimaginatively squared up. Calculated unbalance had been the fashion in her day, and she still felt most at home with it. Ornaments must cluster casually to right or left, never balanced against one another; pictures must not be centred; the podgy conformity of a three-piece suite was blasphemy. Arthur had once said that he felt their living room was in danger of tilting sideways, but he had grown used to it. Brigid had been familiar with this atmosphere all her life, and Nell had tried to contribute something on the same lines to the flat. Mrs Hemming, however, had been brought up in a more conformist school. A mantelpiece should have a clock smack in the middle, and two candlesticks or china figures precisely placed one at each end. She had been shocked to find that there were no mantelpieces in the flat, but she had done her best to adjust its contents to suit her own visual tastes.

Seeing Nell looking around, she said defensively: "I'll be getting packed up in the next day or two."

"There's no hurry. The youngsters won't be back yet."

"I don't want them to feel I'm hanging about. I'll get a room somewhere while I look round."

"Betty, I'm sure they won't mind if . . . "

"They're not going to have me round their necks. Wouldn't be right. I'll find somewhere. I'll tidy this place up and be out of here long before they get back."

It was impossible to believe that it could be any tidier. Nell made a mental resolve to nip in as soon as Mrs Hemming had left and set things to rights again.

It was late afternoon as they made the final return trip to the hotel. Workmen were climbing into a truck at the top of the slope. Arthur and the Borough Surveyor were making a final check over the ground which tomorrow would shudder to the crunch of explosives. A few holiday makers watched from a distance, determined to get as much free entertainment as possible. "Reckon it's going to topple over, eh?" They waited and hoped. One busybody was explaining the whole principle of the job at great length to his family. Two old women waved to Mrs Hemming, who bit her lip and ignored them. Another older woman, tall and very erect, stood to one side, her dark eyes impassive in a dark, lined face. She was not a local, but looked unlike the usual sort of visitor to Lurgate.

Arthur waved to Nell, beckoning her across the terrace. She and Mrs Hemming picked their way warily over the crumbling earth.

"Darling, the damnedest thing. I've got to go over and see old Pinfold."

"Who's he?"

"You know. The vicar — our chum who wants to make a national monument out of that Georgian house. He's just sent a message that he can get all the interested parties together this evening. It may be our only chance to beat them all into submission. I want this thing settled — so don't expect me back till morning."

"Sure it isn't some girl friend you've got tucked away up country?"

"Wish it were. Don't suppose there'll be anyone under the age of seventy there."

"Poor old things, having to face your fury."

"I'm going to get it over with," said Arthur, "if it takes all night. But they'll be a crotchety crowd. I don't fancy driving back in the small hours. I'll settle the cranks, get an early cup of coffee off the Rev., and drive straight to the site here in the morning. One big bang — very satisfying after Pinfold and his chums — and then you can set up some breakfast for me."

"What time's blast-off?"

"Eight o'clock, before most of the tourists surface. We don't want a crowd hanging around inhaling dust."

Mrs Hemming's legs were straddled, her feet planted wide apart. She glared at the hotel as thought to stiffen its will to resist.

"What will it be like? What will happen?"

Arthur smiled sympathetically. When he spoke he was quiet and matter-of-fact. "We set a charge to slice through the foundations over there. We're aiming to bring as much as possible down into the cleft. Then we'll have to cut back the cliff and use the rubble for filling and buttressing it."

"Hm."

"At least you're insured."

"You think I can just start all over again? All that work, building something up — again?"

"No," said Arthur. "I'd say it was time for you to sit back a bit. Now that Martin's off your hands, why not take it easy?"

"I could find a small house. Perhaps let a couple of rooms — nice regular lodgers, respectable folk. Give me something to occupy myself with."

Arthur's gaze strayed to his wrist watch.

Nell said: "We'd better be going. You'll come home first?"

"I can do with a clean-up before I set off."

"There'll be a watchman on duty tonight?" asked Mrs Hemming, seeking to have every detail established in her mind, resenting every last little trickle of her draining control over the hotel.

"No need. We're not leaving any stores around. Don't fancy leaving a stack of explosive for the yobs to play football with at midnight."

"If the hooligans break into the hotel ... "

"I propose to lock up now." Arthur urged them up the slope.

"You?"

"I'm holding the spare set of keys." As she drew breath to protest, he said gently: "I'm the contractor, you know. The place is my responsibility now."

"I see. If you want me to surrender my set ... "

"Of course not."

"That's what we came back for — my keys. I'll just run in and fetch them. I know exactly where they are."

"We'll wait for you," said Nell. Arthur sighed.

"I wouldn't dream of keeping you." Mrs Hemming quickened her pace away from them.

"If you hurry, we can drop you ... "

"I won't have you going all that way round."

Arthur, only too glad to take her at her word, called: "You will lock up behind you, won't you?"

Mrs Hemming did not deign to answer.

She went on into her home for the last time. Arthur slid into the car beside Nell.

Nell said: "I hope she won't do anything . . . I mean, I wouldn't want her to do anything silly."

"Hurl herself from the battlements? She's not the type. Look," said Arthur impatiently as Nell still did not start the engine, "if you're going to fret about her, for goodness' sake go and . . . "

"No," said Nell.

She drove off.

That evening she was restless, unable to settle to anything. Brigid had been gone for some days, and she was just beginning to accept that this was a permanent thing: Brigid was married, belonged somewhere else to somebody else. Arthur was out for the evening and probably for the night. The place was empty.

For Mrs Hemming it was going to be like this always, from now on. Nell had seen more than enough of Betty Hemming for one day, but felt a nagging sense of responsibility towards her.

Perhaps they ought to have a meal

together. Go out somewhere — make the evening pass more quickly.

She telephoned the flat. There was no reply.

It was odd. She must be back by now. Unless she had been unable to find the keys? If, unknown to the rest of them, one of the workmen had spotted the keys and taken them away, Mrs Hemming would be locked out of the flat.

In that case surely she would have come here?

Nell fidgeted round the house. She could not bear to stay in here on her own. She took the car out again and drove a circuitous way into town. It was even more circuitous than she had planned, since police signs had by now commanded a diversion, isolating the road past the hotel. She had to wind her way through a small network of quiet residential side streets, catching just one glimpse of the dark shape of the hotel against the horizon. It look solid and immutable. It was criminal to destroy it.

Mrs Hemming was probably as restless as herself and had decided to eat out. It was unlike her; but so many things today were unlike what they had been yesterday, and tomorrow there would be even more violent changes.

Nell peeped into two restaurants on the off-chance that Mrs Hemming might be in one of them, alone at a table. Then she gave up and had a meal in a quiet place where she and Arthur were fairly well known. She talked to the manager, got home late, and went to bed tired.

Shortly after midnight the telephone rang.

Brigid's voice filtered through a crackle and hiss along the line. "Mummy, where on earth have you been? We tried to ring you from Palermo . . . "

"Palermo?" Muzzily Nell said: "I thought you were supposed to be in Malta."

"We are now. It's a long story. But we're coming home on a plane an hour from now. It's the first one we could wangle on to."

"There's nothing wrong, is there? You and Martin . . . ?"

"It's not us at all. It's Serafina."

"Brigid, really! At this hour of the night."

"Serafina Blythe." Brigid's voice whispered away and then came back again more strongly. "She's still alive. And we think she must be over there in Lurgate. We're worried stiff. You see, now she knows her husband didn't just walk out on her but was murdered, she'll have to pursue the vendetta . . . "

"The what?"

"Vendetta. She'll have to settle up the account. And if the murderer's dead, then his family — or *her* family — comes next on the list."

"I haven't the foggiest idea what you're talking about. Have *you*?"

"Mummy, don't you see? You and Daddy could be in danger. You or Mrs Hemming."

"What's Mrs Hemming got to do with it?"

"The daughter of Serafina's deadly rival. It might have been her mother who killed Walter Blythe. Or Daddy's father. Maybe Serafina doesn't know which it was, so she'll try to deal with all of you — and with Martin and me as well. Though why she had to kill Peter, if it was her, we don't know."

"This is too much."

"Mummy, is Mrs Hemming all right?"

"Of course she's all right."

"When did you last see her?"

"Only a few hours ago. We've been shifting her bits and pieces."

"Martin's been so worried about her. You see, we've been up there, to Serafina's home, and there's such a dreadful atmosphere there. We can just feel that she's up to no good. We're coming home as fast as we can, but Mummy, please be careful, and tell Mrs Hemming . . . "

Two distant, ethereal voices began to argue across the line, then there was a click, a spluttering, and silence.

Nell held the receiver for a few moments, then replaced it. She lay back and waited for another ring. But the line had been a bad one to start with. She had no idea how easy or difficult it was to make a call from Malta to Lurgate.

After ten minutes she put her hand on the receiver.

Mrs Hemming did not care much

for telephone calls even in the daytime, even as part of the inevitable routine of running a hotel, making bookings, ordering food.

Nell let another five minutes go by and then dialled the number of the flat.

There was no reply.

If a workman had taken the keys away, so that Mrs Hemming was unable to let herself into the flat, she might just conceivably have gone off in her stubborn, independent way to find a hotel room. All the same it was odd that she had not contacted Nell.

Unless she felt that this would have been construed as a request for hospitality . . .

Something could have happened to her in Fernrock.

A falling ceiling, a jammed door.

Something.

Nell was wide awake. She turned over and then turned back again. It was ridiculous to worry. There was always a simple, dull explanation to anything. It was only the availability of the telephone that got people so steamed up. Just because you made a call and got no immediate reply, this didn't mean that sinister things were happening. Tomorrow there would be a perfectly mundane explanation.

Such as that Betty Hemming had been trapped in her old home by a falling beam or a collapsing floor.

Nell spent another ten minutes trying to go to sleep. Then she got up and pulled on slacks and a heavy old pullover which had once been emerald green and now had the hue and texture of seaweed. She drove along the familiar route and narrowly avoided smashing through a barrier: she had forgotten the diversion which led her away from the hotel.

In the block of flats, one light shone on each landing level. She rang the doorbell of the flat where Brigid and Martin would live when they got back — and realised that this meant this morning, a few hours from now.

There was no answer. She tried again. After a third attempt she took out her own key and let herself in.

The packages and odds and ends lay on the shelf where Mrs Hemming had dumped them earlier.

Nell went out and drove back the way she had come. She parked the car in a sleeping side street and walked up to the hotel, ducking under one of the barriers.

The hotel still looked solid and imposing.

There was a torch in the car, she remembered. It needed a new battery, but it was still in working order. She ought to go back and get it.

No real need, she told herself. She wasn't going to do anything silly. She had no intention of prowling round the deserted hotel. She would go up to the front door, make sure it was locked, and then go away again.

She reached the front door and tried the handle.

The door opened.

Nell stood frozen for a moment, then went in. Betty Hemming could not have found her keys . . . could not have locked the door behind her.

Then why . . . ?

Nell stepped warily into the stripped, echoing hall, with the reception desk bare and unwelcoming, the staircase a faint shadow ahead of her. No lights, no carpet, no warmth.

"Mrs Hemming," she called. Her voice

rose, then came seeping back to her. "Betty? Mrs Hemming?"

Somewhere there was a sound. Not just the echo of her own voice but a murmur, a voice and a rustle of movement; and then silence which somehow emphasised what she had half-heard.

Nell went step by step towards the staircase.

"Betty . . . ?"

The hollow echo of her voice mocked her. On the first landing she took a cigarette lighter from the pocket of her slacks. Its tiny flame picked out a row of doors. Bedrooms on the left, she recalled, facing the sea. On the right, bathrooms, two lavatories, and a linen room.

One of the doors on the right was ajar. Nell pushed it and went in.

There was the faint thud of the door closing behind her, and the squeak of a key in the lock. She spun round, and looked into a dark face etched darker by the hazy, fluttering light.

The woman said in a deep, aged, masculine voice: "I do not think you will know who I am."

There was only one woman it could

possibly be. But Nell, stalling, said absurdly: "No, I don't think we've met."

"You look for your friend."

"She's here, then?" Nell glanced back at the door. "If she's ill . . . had an accident . . . get a doctor . . . "

"I think you do not leave." A knife gleamed from the woman's hand like a long, wicked claw. "We stay here. And I tell you who I am, so you know why things will be as they must be."

15

TRAYS were slid on to the flimsy tables in front of them. Brigid moved her book to one side.

"Tea or coffee?"

"Coffee," said Brigid although they had already drunk two large cups at the airport. Her face was dry, her hands sticky.

She knew the key passages of the book off by heart. As the minutes ticked by and the plane vibrated and occasionally tilted gently, the sentences became clamorous in her head.

The style of writing was florid and melodramatic, but this suited the subject all too well. Sicily had always been an island of violence and flamboyant postures. For centuries it had been the custom for the widow of a murdered man to swear vengeance on the killer. If she had sons, they must work with her to wipe out the stain. If she was alone, it was still her duty to pit herself against the murderer and his entire family. At the time the book was written, vendetta had been an accepted practice. In the supposedly enlightened nineteen-sixties it might be carried on rather more covertly, but Brigid thought it unlikely that enlightenment had gone as far as to ban it altogether. The younger folk might long to flee to the emancipation of the cities and to other countries, and some might succeed; but those who had to stay behind would come in time to accept the customs of their parents as surely as any young couple in a Streatham semi-detached. The code of family convention was one thing in Streatham, another in Sicily; but just as immutable and inescapable.

Brigid sipped her coffee and turned a page of the book.

"Men of respect" — that was the phrase. Men of respect and women of honour.

Serafina had believed that her husband had deserted her. He had embezzled his own firm's money and vanished. She had returned to her home town in full widow's panoply and remained there until the revelation came that Walter Blythe had been murdered. Then it became her duty to return to England and settle this deadly account.

Yet how had she been able to live in such high style in Manciano? It fitted the story she had told the townspeople, but not the story as it now stood. Nobody had suspected that she was not what she claimed to be: the rich widow of the English businessman who had met her on holiday, married her and set her up in England, and left her all his money when he died. What was one to suspect now?

The money . . .

Had there been something between her and the Johnson partner, Brigid's grandfather? Had he, the supposed embezzler in the latest version of the story, paid her off to keep her quiet?

And if so, where did this much vaunted Sicilian family honour come into it? There was no mention in the book Brigid had been reading of people allowing themselves to be bought off. If a Johnson had killed Serafina's husband and Serafina knew it, then or now, it was her bounden duty to harry the Johnsons.

Brigid shivered in spite of the enervating heat of the plane.

But there had been no sign of the Johnsons being attacked at any time, past or present. The Hemmings, yes; and Peter . . . Pietro.

Could it . . . no, she mustn't think it, yet kept thinking it . . . could Peter have been killed by Mrs Hemming?

Her cup was empty. The stewardess came past with the coffee-pot raised. Brigid shook her head and sat back, closing her eyes.

It was difficult to get things in the right order. This was a disability they had suffered when talking to the girl in Manciano. To fill in details of events before she was born, the girl had brought her father into the discussion. He had been a hindrance rather than a help. He was suspicious of strangers and their motives, and in his presence the girl herself became vague and incoherent, seeming to fear that by some sixth sense he might understand the English words and cut her short in mid-sentence. Her disjointed phrases and implications came in a thickening accent which made them even harder to interpret.

But she was pathetically eager to keep on the good side of the visitors. Twice she asked if she could visit them in England, if she came to England; if they could tell her *how* to come to England and to be allowed to stay there.

Serafina — this at any rate was clear — had played her arrogant role in Manciano for as long as anyone could remember. Feared and respected in the community, she had been taken at her own valuation. Then news of the discovery of Walter Blythe's corpse was brought by Pietro, complete with newspapers and illustrated magazines — Pietro, the spoilt grandson, the compulsive talker, the opportunist. It was known that there had been furious arguments between his grandmother and himself, perhaps because he had been the one to publicise the juicy news in Manciano, or perhaps because he was demanding money for himself and telling her how to get it.

Then Pietro went away again. Had they come to some arrangement: had she sent him as her emissary to claim money from the Johnsons, not wishing to reveal her own existence? But, wondered Brigid, if she had been too proud to accept money from the Johnsons half a century ago, why was she prepared to take it now?

Because in those far-off days she hadn't known that her husband had been murdered by a Johnson.

That might fit. But if Pietro-Peter had been her emissary, why had she suddenly set off for England herself, a little later, and killed him . . . killed her own grandson?

If it had really been Serafina who killed him. *If* . . .

Brigid opened her eyes as the stewardess removed the tray, and saw that Martin was looking sideways at her with a rueful, affectionate smile.

He said: "Rather a short honeymoon."

"Do you think we're being stupid?"

"We'd be stupid not to go back. We'd never have been easy in our minds if we'd stayed."

The engine note changed. Brigid thought gladly that they must be almost there, then saw from her watch that they couldn't be. She yawned, and found that her ears had been blocked up.

Still trying to sort out the questions which had been buzzing behind her closed eyes, she offered one or two to Martin, not very hopefully.

"Why did Serafina make a set for you or your mother rather than for us, the Johnsons? Did she know something that we don't?"

"If she did, she still knows it — and we still don't."

"And all that money. Living it up richly all those years. Suppose . . . just suppose . . . that it was Walter Blythe who really did embezzle the money, and not my grandfather at all. Perhaps he had to: perhaps your grandmother was blackmailing him, or something. And Serafina found out, and he had to pay her off as well. So . . . "

"So?"

"Oh, dear. It's getting in such a tangle. I feel as though I'm doing a lot of complicated knitting in my head, and it's all got snarled up."

They sat in silence for a while. The plane hung infuriatingly in space, making no discernible progress. Brigid braced her feet against the floor, urging it on.

Martin put his hand over hers.

"We're probably worrying needlessly. Building up a great big drama out of nothing."

"Nothing?" cried Brigid so loudly that the head of a man drowsing in the seat in front of her jerked in protest. "One corpse in the old house, one corpse under the pier . . . and that woman prowling around Lurgate, and you call it nothing?"

At the airport Martin plunged into arrangements for hiring a self-drive car. The advertisements made it sound simple and enticing, but in reality the formalities produced an exasperating delay.

Brigid filled in the time by making two telephone calls.

Alarm mounted when she got no reply to the first one. The ringing tone went on and on in her parents' house. She knew the extension in the bedroom couldn't fail to wake her mother and father if they were in.

If they were in . . . and alive.

On and on it went, and there was no reassuring answer.

She tried the flat. Mrs Hemming might

take some time to get to the phone, but if it rang for long enough she would surely, grumbling, reach it.

Brigid let it ring and ring. Nothing here, either.

Martin came back. "Honestly, I thought they were going to ask to inspect my birthmarks and take my fingerprints. Get through all right?"

"No," said Brigid. "Not to either of them."

"Perhaps they're . . . " But there was no easy, ready-made explanation. He said: "Come on, then."

They drove out into the pallid dawn, racing down the long miles towards Lurgate.

16

THE floor of the linen room was hard and cold. A candle stuck upright from the bare boards between Nell and Serafina. Its flame did not waver. The linen room had no window, and its door fitted too well to allow any draughts in. It was all of a piece with Mrs Hemming's devotion to the ultimate respectability of silence: neither she nor her guests must be distracted by the chatter and laughter of maids thumping about in here.

Serafina said: "I am sorry you had to walk in here, Mrs Johnson. So very sorry. Because of course it is not possible you walk out again. You understand?"

Squatting uncomfortably on the bleak floor, Nell watched the blade of the knife winking wickedly in the candlelight.

"You can't keep me here for ever."

"It will not be for ever. In the morning there will be an end."

"You don't imagine I'm just going to

sit here and let myself be blown up? As soon as the workmen arrive ... "

"They will hear nothing. You scream, they do not hear."

"There's not just me. Mrs Hemming ... "

"They will not hear her."

A cold more savage than the night chill bit into Nell's bones. She said: "What have you done to her? Is she ... alive?"

"It is fitting," said Serafina complacently, "that she perish in the ruins of her home."

"You're mad."

In the miserable glow, the face hardened into the set ferocity of a mask from a totem pole.

"I have done what had to be done. You will not go alone. I stay with you. The duty is done, and I am happy to go with you."

"If I'm going to die anyway" — it sounded terrible and incredible, put into words, and Nell tried to keep her voice from shaking — "I may as well fight it out with you. Now or later."

"I am old," said Serafina, "but I am still strong. Strong enough to deal with Pietro as he deserved."

"So it was you. You killed your own grandson."

"Better so. There is nobody else who must carry the weight of it. Pietro defied me. He stole from me. I have told you, I am Serafina Blythe, and from me my grandson he stole all what was left of my life. My life with Walter Blythe. He steal my possessions and bring them to England so he make the easy money. That was Pietro. It could not be permitted."

"You came after him all that way just to . . . well, to . . . "

"I follow him, yes. We meet in the street. I remember these streets. There are changes, but not so many. I know where to go. I meet him, and he is afraid to see me. If he had come to me then and begged forgiveness, perhaps I spare him. But he ran away, and when we meet again he is drunk."

"That must have been after he took money from my husband." Nell laughed mirthlessly. "Celebrating!"

"I tell him what the end must be. He cries and he argues. But there is nothing he can do. He is weak. It was the English blood in him," said Serafina. "All he can do is to cry. And then to taunt me." Her features became more and more those of a destructive spirit, to be placated only by sacrifice. "He say the vile things, he spit the wicked things in my face."

"What things?"

"This I do not permit. And the money — I will not permit that. The Johnsons, they are nothing to me. They were never anything. I have told you. I am sorry you are here and I cannot let you go. But it is not right I should be dishonoured by my grandson. I do not permit Pietro to take money from you falsely."

"Falsely?" Nell almost let it pass, weaving its ragged way in and out of the other threads of nightmare. Then, grasping it, she said: "Do you mean Pietro had no right to the money — that he wasn't Walter's grandson?"

"He was Walter's grandson," said Serafina fiercely.

"Then . . . Why were you so upset about the money? Didn't you feel *you* were entitled to come forward and claim some of it? You and he — the last surviving members of the family. What was *false* about the claim?"

Serafina's hooded eyes stared down into the candle flame. It swayed gently and bent away from her as though she had breathed a suffocating breath on it.

There was nothing to lose now. Nell lashed out with words like weapons; words barbed and excoriating.

"You say he taunted you. What did he say? What did he know about you that made you so angry? Only the truth," she cried, "can make people angry enough to kill."

"He is dead now. The debt is paid."

"What did he say that you didn't want to hear?"

"Soon it will all be ended."

Nell saw a blaze of scorching truth at the end of the dark dream. She said:

"It was *you*!"

"I killed Pietro. I have said this. I do not deny it."

"I'm not talking about Pietro." Nell leaned forward. There was the faintest warmth from the flame, some way below her chin. "You wouldn't accept money from the Johnsons, would you? Wouldn't accept it ever. Didn't take it in the past when Walter had disappeared, and didn't accept my husband's offer when Walter showed up again. Your honour, your pride, or whatever this thing of yours is — it wouldn't let you touch a penny, would it? Why? Because you weren't entitled to it," Nell went recklessly on. "Because you knew from the start that Walter hadn't walked out on you, and because you knew then and now that it wasn't a Johnson who'd had anything to do with the mess-up. It wasn't a Johnson who killed Walter. You knew that. And how could you have known it?"

When she paused, the silence seemed to thicken and close in on her. The knife lay loosely across Serafina's palm. Nell wondered whether she dared risk a sudden leap; but there was no strength in her legs.

"You could only be so sure," said Nell, "if you'd killed Walter yourself. And you did, didn't you? It was you who killed Walter Blythe."

Serafina said very softly: "Why should I kill my husband?"

"Because he wasn't your husband. How long did it take you to find that out? How long to realise that Walter had led you up the garden path — that he'd gone through some marriage ritual which had no legal or religious validity at all?"

Serafina's face looked for the first time human and pitiful. But her grip on the knife tightened. She eased it into a new position of readiness.

She said: "When men lie to their women, they must die."

"Mrs Hemming was telling the truth. Walter Blythe really was married to her mother. He deserted her, but she found him and they came together again. Literally together again — so that she became pregnant."

"A daughter!" snarled Serafina. "*I* had a son."

"But you didn't know about that in time, did you? Walter was already on the rebound, back to his Welsh girl again."

"She was cheap." Again Serafina's breath lashed the flame into an agitated dance. "A nothing, a silly little nothing. But Walter was so weak. It was all there again, all the weakness and the wrong, in Pietro."

"The money," Nell hazarded. "the

money he embezzled . . . "

Of course. She didn't even need to catechise Serafina. The whole thing had been organised so that Walter could run off with his Eiluned. Walter was a great runner, surrendering to his impulses and dodging his responsibilities. By now he must have been regretting Serafina's existence. He ought not to have set her up so pretentiously in Lurgate as his beautiful tempestuous showpiece of a wife. Her Sicilian temperament, so intoxicating at first, must surely have clashed with everything else in the workaday life of an English seaside town. And for all that Latin passion, she had given him no children. He found his real wife to his liking once more, and was delighted when she told him she was expecting a child.

Aloud she said: "He didn't tell you he was legally married to somebody else and wanted to go back to her? Didn't offer some sort of . . . er . . . settlement to you?"

Serafina laughed contemptuously. "Walter? I tell you, he was weak. So afraid."

Nell was not sure that she blamed him.

So Walter must have coaxed Eiluned into being patient while he sorted out his problems. On all the evidence he must have been a great coaxer, a sly and persuasive talker — a fixer, as ever there was. And it was easier to get round Eiluned than round Serafina. With Serafina, the only safe thing to do was disappear once and for all.

But Serafina found out. Serafina killed Walter, buried him, collected the loot he had been hoping to run off with, and returned to respectable retirement in her home town. For years she had walked a tightrope without fear, keeping her audience spellbound by her own unfaltering control. It must have been a shock when she learned that Walter's corpse had risen from the ground; and worse, perhaps, to read the guesses and distortions in the papers which now reached Manciano, to hear the mockery in the town as her pretensions crumbled, and not to be able ever to answer with the truth.

"That's why you killed Pietro," Nell mused. "Not just because of abstract justice or the family code of ethics or what have you. His taunts were the worst of the lot. He'd guessed, hadn't he? By the time you reached Lurgate he had worked it all out. From what Mrs Hemming came out with he deduced that you were never really, legally married to Walter. And from there on it wasn't hard to see that you must have been Walter's killer. Where else could your money have come from? It had to be you. And he laughed at you . . . "

"Be quiet."

"Laughed," said Nell, "about your rival, and your high opinion of yourself, and his father's illegitimacy, and your own theft of Walter's embezzled money — after all the high-sounding principles you'd laid down to *him*! — and about . . . "

"You will be quiet, I have said." The blade of the knife jutted outwards. "You will not speak like this. To me, no."

"And it was you who tried to kill Martin, with a do-it-yourself avalanche and then with a knife."

"The knife was for the child of shame. For *her*." Serafina jerked her head towards the door. The gesture had no direction and no real meaning in this doomed, silent, deserted hotel. "But it is her child who comes . . . and I am content he should go first. It is a pity, I do not have the time. I make the mistake. He is still alive."

Nell said: "Where's Mrs Hemming?"

"A few hours and we shall all be the same, all together."

"You kill all three of us, and somehow that evens up the score — honour satisfied and all that?"

"As you say. Yes. Without honour there is nothing to live for, or die for."

"It's barbaric."

"I tell you, Mrs Johnson, it is not my wish you are here. I like to let you go. But I do not think you promise to speak to nobody. And if you promise, I do not think you keep it. You are English, and the English have no honour."

Nell tried to estimate how long the candle would take to gutter down. In darkness, what chance would she stand against this fearsome old woman with a knife?

She could blow it out now, suddenly, and jump.

Or she could sit here and wait and work out exactly what she proposed to do.

Again she asked: "Where's Mrs Hemming?"

This time Serafina did not bother to make any reply.

There was no sound. Nell would not have believed it possible to insulate a room so effectively from the outside world. To be so close to the sea and for there to be none of that steady background grumble which people in Lurgate took so much for granted; to hear no traffic, not even a rackety motor-bike racing out of the town . . .

"It seems so futile to me," she said. "I mean, you can't set the past to rights: it's fixed, you can't undo it. And you can't stop the future happening."

"I make sure there is no future for Walter Blythe's daughter."

"And what does that gain you? It's not Betty Hemming's fault her mother was Walter's legal wife."

Serafina flinched as she must have flinched when Peter jeered his insults at her.

She said venomously: "My son is dead. I have had to take the life of my grandson. Now that woman's daughter, too, must die. That is the only justice. Then it is finished . . . finished . . . *finished!*"

"But it *won't* be finished," said Nell. "There's Mrs Hemming's son. And then there'll be his children." Brigid's children, she thought with a pang of loss for what she would never see. Fury snapped and tore within her. "Don't you see how mad it is — how pointless?"

Serafina flicked her left hand derisively as though to dismiss this point. Then it fell slowly back into her lap. She hunched up, brooding.

No, thought Nell. Oh, God, no. What have I said? What idea have I put into that twisted mind?

Serafina nodded.

Nell said feverishly: "The whole thing's a ghastly aberration. Right from the start. Can't you see that? You can't go on and on for ever, so . . . "

"But yes," said Serafina. "For ever and ever. You must go on. That is vendetta."

She began to stand up. Nell, fighting against cramp in her legs and fear in her heart, tried to rise at the same time. The knife at once flicked towards her throat.

"You stay," said Serafina. "And I thank you. I am lazy, I wish to give up and sleep — but you are right, you tell me my duty. So I leave the hotel and I wait. When the hotel is gone, I wait for your daughter and her husband to come home."

"You can't," cried Nell. "You can't just . . ."

"Do not fear. I will not harm your daughter. Only him. They come back in about a week, I think?"

Nell gulped. "Yes."

"Perhaps when they hear you are found in the ruins here, they come sooner. But I think they do not know I am waiting here. It will be a surprise to him, also, to know that Serafina is still alive."

Nell could trust herself only to nod.

"I think," said Serafina, "he will not have the time to recover from this surprise." She stood erect, looking down with stern compassion on Nell. "And now . . . before I leave, I must see you are . . . safe." The word seemed to amuse her. "Safe," she chuckled to herself.

17

THE barriers were new. Driving fast up a road he knew well, accelerating over the last lap in the hope of finding reassurance at the end of it, Martin had to brake hard. He followed a diversion sign into a quiet side street.

They were halfway down it when Brigid let out a gasp.

"Mummy's car!"

They stopped beside it and looked in. There was no way of telling how long it had been standing in this street.

"Your mother might be staying the night with friends. If there's anyone here you know . . . "

"There isn't. I'm sure we don't know anybody living up here. Anyway, she wouldn't have got out of bed at midnight and come visiting."

Martin slid the car gently forward and prepared to turn at the corner along the diversionary route. Then he said: "Wait a minute. This route — it can only be to steer traffic away from the hotel."

"Something must have happened. We ought to go and look."

"After we've checked on your mother."

"No." Brigid remembered what her mother had said about shifting Mrs Hemming's bits and pieces. But that had been in the afternoon. They would surely not have gone back in the small hours. It made no sense. All the same . . . "Turn back up this next road. Get as close as you can. We've got to go and see."

She was grateful to him for not arguing. It was not that he was meekly taking orders; simply that he responded to her sense of urgency, and acted.

They parked the car and hurried along the pavement past one of the barriers. A policeman stepped across the Fernrock entrance as they approached. He raised an imperious hand, then recognised them. "Oh. You, Mr Martin. Thought you was away on honeymoon, like."

"Have you seen my mother go in there?" asked Brigid. "Or Mrs Hemming?"

"Not this morning, I haven't. Only the workmen so far."

"Workmen?"

"Getting set to blow it up. Not safe any longer."

Martin's breath hissed in between his teeth.

Brigid said: "My father, then? He's here?"

"Not yet, miss. Due along any minute, though."

Martin took her arm and began to march her forward. To the policeman he said: "Tell Mr Johnson we'll meet him down there."

"Well, I don't know ... " They were on their way. The policeman raised his voice. "Stay well clear of the house, now. Way over the side of the slope."

They circled the hotel and came out on the top terrace. Men were unrolling a length of thin cable. The foreman came past, a few feet away from Brigid. He looked startled to see her there.

Brigid said: "You're sure there's nobody in there?"

"Indoors there? Not likely. Had a proper clear-out yesterday. Place locked up. No, miss — no visititors having a free kip."

Martin went towards the front door. Brigid followed the foreman indignantly on her heels.

The door was securely fastened.

"Now, look here, Miss Johnson . . . "

"Mrs Hemming."

"Eh? Oh, yes, o' course. Sorry. But anyways, your Dad wouldn't be too pleased if you was to get a slate on your head, now, would he?"

Hankey, the Borough Surveyor, appeared behind them. Brigid gabbled out her disjointed story of the telephone calls, the one that had got through and the others that hadn't. They must, must have a last-minute check through the building.

Hankey tried the door. "Your mother," he said to Martin, "was one of the last to leave. She was asked to lock up behind her. Evidently she did."

Martin felt in his jacket pocket. "I've still got a key to the side door — our own rooms."

"We can't have anyone prowling round inside."

"There's something wrong somewhere," said Martin. "You've got to hold off blasting until I've had a proper look. Don't worry — I know every inch of the place."

Before Hankey could protest, Martin went under the shadow of the trees towards the secluded side door.

Brigid was about to go after him when a car turned cautiously in from the road and stopped well back from the hotel. Her father got out. He stared, thunderstruck.

"You're supposed to be in Malta."

"You haven't talked to Mummy? She hasn't told you?"

"Told me what?"

"We phoned her last night and tried to tell her . . . "

"I've been out all night. On some Georgian tiles. Trying to keep them securely where they belong."

"Where *is* Mummy, then?"

"At home in bed, I shouldn't wonder. Or having a solitary breakfast in peace."

"She's not," said Brigid. "We tried to ring her from the airport, and she's not there. Nor is Martin's mother. Daddy, you've got to stop operations on this hotel until we've gone right through it."

"Look, if you imagine I'm going to lose

time and money . . . "

"Serafina," said Brigid. "Serafina Blythe. Does that mean anything to you? She's still alive, and we think she's right here in Lurgate, and we think Mrs Hemming might be in danger. And where's Mummy?"

It came out jumbled and unbalanced. She finished by pounding her fists against her father's chest. He held her off at arm's length, trying to laugh but seeing how serious it must be to her. "All right, all right. We'll go through the place. Top to bottom. And I'll bet your mother and Mrs Hemming will have something to say when they hear about it."

He went down the slope to issue instructions, then came back swinging a bunch of keys from his little finger. The door opened. Light fell across the bare hall. No memory now of holidays and happiness; only the echo of their footsteps as they went towards the stairs.

Brigid raised her voice. "Mummy! Mrs Hemming!"

There was no reply. She tried again, then began to go up the stairs.

A door creaked. They stopped.

Martin came out of the reception office below and looked up. "Fine. You cover the first floor while I go through the rooms down here."

Brigid suppressed a tremor and went on to the landing. She walked along it and called again, and again. Was there a mutter, a faint shuffling sound somewhere, or was it just the wind stirring through the empty rooms?

Her father was flinging doors open brusquely, anxious to prove that she was wasting his time. Brigid tried the doors on the inside of the passage. She looked into the bleak, stripped bathrooms, and into the lavatories.

One door was locked.

"This one won't open," she said over her shoulder.

"Probably jammed. The building's shifted quite a bit."

"I'm sure it's locked."

"Mrs Hemming probably took me too literally and went through the place locking every door that took her fancy."

"Then why not the rooms on your side?" Brigid moved away, then turned back. "Daddy, please. There must be a master key on that bunch you've got."

He tried three before he found the right one. The door swung inwards. Shadows lay beyond the dim swathe of daylight.

"Nell! Oh, my God, Nell . . . "

They both stumbled towards the slatted shelves on which linen had once been heaped.

Brigid's mother was suspended face down from the lowest shelf, her stomach a few inches off the floor. Her wrists and ankles had been tightly lashed to the slats with strips cut from her slacks. Brigid sobbed as she tore at the knots. They lowered the weight gently, and carried Nell out into the corridor.

"Arthur. But it's not. Can't be. Arthur . . . "

"My love." He cradled her against him, rocked her to and fro.

Brigid said desperately: "Mummy, where's Mrs Hemming?"

"She's . . . don't know." The words slurred out. "Don't know. Don't even know if . . . if she's alive." All at once Nell cracked into a hysterical whimper. She abandoned herself to tears and clung to her husband's shoulders. Then she steadied herself. "Where's Martin?"

"Somewhere downstairs," said Brigid. "It's a wonder he didn't hear us. He came in through their old rooms . . . "

"But Serafina was going out that way. She'll be hanging about. She . . . " Nell's voice rose in a howl. "It's Martin she's after now!"

Brigid left them without a backward glance. She ran to the head of the stairs and down, calling as she went. "Martin — Martin, where are you?"

He was not in the hall, and not in the reception office. Their old private rooms were empty. The side door was open.

The trees and the sheltering wall beyond obscured most of the view from here. Far down the slope a workman sat on a heap of rubble, contemplating the horizon. In the opposite direction Brigid glimpsed a brief segment of road, with a few faces peering over the hedge. Some holidaymakers had apparently thought it worth the effort of getting up here early to see the display.

Martin stepped out from the corner of the hotel into a patch of morning sunlight. He must, she realised, have opened the french windows from the lower lounge and let himself out into the garden that way, finishing his tour of the ground floor.

She opened her mouth to call him.

A dark shape moved from the shadows of the trees.

Serafina paced the few yards down the narrow path. Her head jutted forward. There was a terrible sinewy energy in her progress. She was stalking Martin with an incredulous joy — whatever else might be going wrong, here at least was Martin, a ready prey.

He turned to face her.

Faintly Brigid heard Serafina say: "You can help me, please? I stay here and I leave some property, and now what do I see?" One naive, feeble hand waved up at the building. "There is all this work, and nobody inside. Perhaps you tell me . . . "

Her other hand was lost in the folds of a dress too sombre and old-fashioned to be right in Lurgate at this season of the year.

She and Martin were close now. Brigid wanted to cry out, but the sound gagged in her throat. And then she saw from the way Martin stood that he knew the threat and was waiting for it. This could only be Serafina.

She took a step forward, leaning confidingly towards him. There was a shrill dazzle against the sky as the knife blade slashed into the sunlight.

Martin spun on one heel and deftly knocked Serafina's elbow upwards. She let out an ugly shriek and stumbled a couple of steps down the slope. The knife described a parabola in the air and descended further down, bouncing over the rocks.

Martin walked towards her. There were shouts from the far side of the terraces. Two workmen began to make their way across at an angle.

Brigid ran out into the open.

Serafina shrank from the huntress into a creature hunted. She jerked her head this way and that, her eyes counting them all and hating them as they converged on her.

She ran.

She ran along a wild zig-zag course, down a few feet and along the retaining wall of one terrace, then up towards the far side of the hotel, where the drive swept round to the head of the gardens. One of the workmen changed course and went scrambling after her.

Martin halted, panting. Brigid fell against him and clung to him.

"If we let her go, she'll never give up! If she gets away . . . "

A truck backed slowly and warily round the end of the building. Serafina seemed to be racing towards its massive back wheels.

Somebody yelled.

The truck lurched and swung madly to one side to avoid Serafina. It thumped heavily against the corner of the hotel. Serafina, not more than a foot behind it, wavered, looked desperately round, and slithered back a few paces.

The crack down the façade of the hotel widened as though cleft from above by an axe. A ragged pillar of brick and woodwork rocked outwards and stood poised for an interminable second; and then it crumpled down the slope very slowly and majestically. The truck rocked but stayed firm. Bricks came apart, there was a rending and splintering of wood and glass.

Serafina looked up only once, and any sound she might have made was lost in the concussion as the fragments crashed down on her and on the terraces. Dust rose in a great cloud, drifting across the garden, settling on grass and the torn flowerbeds and the men crouching low to the ground.

Arthur Johnson and the Borough Surveyor hurried two women out of the main door and steadied them on the drive outside — Nell leaning on Arthur, and Mrs Hemming doubled up, coughing and retching.

Dust swirled up on the breeze, stinging their eyes.

It was some time before anyone could see where to start digging for Serafina.

On the mangled corpse they found the key to Room twenty-two of Fernrock Hotel. They also found a smeared cheque folded in two, its edges almost tacked together by sea water.

When the police had found the boarding house in which she had been staying,

Detective-Sergeant Campbell was able to report that in her suitcase were all the souvenirs which Peter had produced as credentials and which she had subsequently reclaimed from Room twenty-two.

"So," said Nell, "at least there's an alternative set of theories for the gossips of Lurgate to amuse themselves with."

Arthur nodded. "Nicer if we could have had a signed confession, or set her up in the dock to answer a lot of awkward questions — get it cleared up in public — but it's better than us being the only ones to carry the weight of rumour."

They were sitting in what Brigid tried to think of as her new home. But the tempo and feeling of the place had been established by Mrs Hemming. She brought in a tray of cups and saucers, refusing help. With her knee she nudged a low table into place, equidistant between the divan where Brigid and Martin sat and the chairs where Nell and Arthur had settled.

Martin said "Mum, do take it easy."

"It won't hurt me to make myself

useful. Now that awful business is all over, maybe we can talk some sense and get things sorted out properly."

"All over," mused Arthur. "Mm. All over? Apart from the nasty decaying smell left behind." Abruptly he turned to Nell and added: "Who's for getting out?"

Brigid winked at Martin. "Go North, young man."

Her father said: "What's that?" Then he laughed. "Don't tell me you, too . . . " He made an impulsive gesture towards Martin and succeeded in jolting the teapot as Mrs Hemming tilted it to pour. Tea splashed across the carpet. "You're seriously thinking . . . ?"

They both began to talk at once. About new cities and old traditions, about buildings and about bugs, about construction and research and imagination. About getting out of Lurgate.

Nell managed to get a word in at last. "There have been Johnsons in Lurgate since goodness knows when. Are you sure you can bear to leave?" Her hand rested on the arm of the chair. Arthur touched it lightly. "Are you sure?" she insisted.

Mrs Hemming kept an eye on people's

untrustworthy arms and elbows, and poured with a steady hand into the row of cups she had arranged symmetrically along the table.

"Down with ancestors," said Martin. "Look what they did to that poor woman, Serafina."

"Poor woman!" snorted his mother.

"Family pride. Family spitefulness. You can never balance that kind of ledger. Write it off and get out. Start again."

Arthur was looking earnestly at Nell. "You think you could stand it?"

"Anyone would think we were talking about the North Pole. Why shouldn't I be able to stand it?"

"It's all right for me. All right to work there, I mean. But not much fun for you. Can't guarantee you the sort of place you'd choose to live in."

"Isn't the basic idea that you're going to make the places worth living in?"

"It won't be achieved for some years. A generation, maybe."

"I'd like to be there," said Nell, "when you make a start." Her lips twitched. "What are we arguing about, anyway? I know when you've made up your mind.

There's only one thing I dread. I'm not sure I can face it."

Brigid edged closer to Martin. Whatever the objections, she and Martin were going. Martin wanted it that way, so she wanted it too. She waited.

"It's the electricity," said Nell.

"What's electricity got to do with it?" Arthur demanded.

"Think of the power points. All those plugs and sockets, that kind of thing. They're bound to be different, wherever we go. They always are."

They began to laugh, and Mrs Hemming shrugged and said "Well, I don't know, I'm sure," and the men leaned towards each other across the table and began to talk to and at and over each other, planning an escape as though there were not a second to lose.

Craning round Arthur's head, Nell smiled at Brigid. "They're both crazy."

"Yes," said Brigid happily, "they are, aren't they?"

CLOUD OVER MALVERTON
Nancy Buckingham

Dulcie soon realises that something is seriously wrong at Malverton, and when violence strikes she is horrified to find herself under suspicion of murder.

AFTER THOUGHTS
Max Bygraves

The Cockney entertainer tells stories of his East End childhood, of his RAF days, and his post-war showbusiness successes and friendships with fellow comedians.

MOONLIGHT AND MARCH ROSES
D. Y. Cameron

Lynn's search to trace a missing girl takes her to Spain, where she meets Clive Hendon. While untangling the situation, she untangles her emotions and decides on her own future.

THE TWILIGHT MAN
Frank Gruber

Jim Rand lives alone in the California desert awaiting death. Into his hermit existence comes a teenage girl who blows both his past and his brief future wide open.

DOG IN THE DARK
Gerald Hammond

Jim Cunningham breeds and trains gun dogs, and his antagonism towards the devotees of show spaniels earns him many enemies. So when one of them is found murdered, the police are on his doorstep within hours.

THE RED KNIGHT
Geoffrey Moxon

When he finds himself a pawn on the chessboard of international espionage with his family in constant danger, Guy Trent becomes embroiled in moves and countermoves which may mean life or death for Western scientists.

THE LISTERDALE MYSTERY
Agatha Christie

Twelve short stories ranging from the light-hearted to the macabre, diverse mysteries ingeniously and plausibly contrived and convincingly unravelled.

TO BE LOVED
Lynne Collins

Andrew married the woman he had always loved despite the knowledge that Sarah married him for reasons of her own. So much heartache could have been avoided if only he had known how vital it was to be loved.

ACCUSED NURSE
Jane Converse

Paula found herself accused of a crime which could cost her her job, her nurse's reputation, and even the man she loved, unless the truth came to light.

BUTTERFLY MONTANE
Dorothy Cork

Parma had come to New Guinea to marry Alec Rivers, but she found him completely disinterested and that overbearing Pierce Adams getting entirely the wrong idea about her.

HONOURABLE FRIENDS
Janet Daley

Priscilla Burford is happily married when she meets Junior Environment Minister Alistair Thurston. Inevitably, sexual obsession and political necessity collide.

WANDERING MINSTRELS
Mary Delorme

Stella Wade's career as a concert pianist might have been ruined by the rudeness of a famous conductor, so it seemed to her agent and benefactor. Even Sir Nicholas fails to see the possibilities when John Tallis falls deeply in love with Stella.

MORNING IS BREAKING
Lesley Denny

The growing frenzy of war catapults Diane Clements into a clandestine marriage and separation with a German refugee.

LAST BUS TO WOODSTOCK
Colin Dexter

A girl's body is discovered huddled in the courtyard of a Woodstock pub, and Detective Chief Inspector Morse and Sergeant Lewis are hunting a rapist and a murderer.

THE STUBBORN TIDE
Anne Durham

Everyone advised Carol not to grieve so excessively over her cousin's death. She might have followed their advice if the man she loved thought that way about her, but another girl came first in his affections.

A GREAT DELIVERANCE
Elizabeth George

Into the web of old houses and secrets of Keldale Valley comes Scotland Yard Inspector Thomas Lynley and his assistant to solve a particularly savage murder.

'E' IS FOR EVIDENCE
Sue Grafton

Kinsey Millhone was bogged down on a warehouse fire claim. It came as something of a shock when she was accused of being on the take. She'd been set up. Now she had a new client — herself.

A FAMILY OUTING IN AFRICA
Charles Hampton and Janie Hampton

A tale of a young family's journey through Central Africa by bus, train, river boat, lorry, wooden bicycle and foot.

SEASONS OF MY LIFE
Hannah Hauxwell and Barry Cockcroft

The story of Hannah Hauxwell's struggle to survive on a desolate farm in the Yorkshire Dales with little money, no electricity and no running water.

TAKING OVER
Shirley Lowe and Angela Ince

A witty insight into what happens when women take over in the boardroom and their husbands take over chores, children and chickenpox.

AFTER MIDNIGHT STORIES,
The Fourth Book Of

A collection of sixteen of the best of today's ghost stories, all different in style and approach but all combining to give the reader that special midnight shiver.

DEAD SPIT
Janet Edmonds

Government vet Linus Rintoul attempts to solve a mystery which plunges him into the esoteric world of pedigree dogs, murder and terrorism, and Crufts Dog Show proves to be far more exciting than he had bargained for . . .

A BARROW IN THE BROADWAY
Pamela Evans

Adopted by the Gordillo family, Rosie Goodson watched their business grow from a street barrow to a chain of supermarkets. But passion, bitterness and her unhappy marriage aliented her from them.

THE GOLD AND THE DROSS
Eleanor Farnes

Lorna found it hard to make ends meet for herself and her mother and then by chance she met two men — one a famous author and one a rich banker. But could she really expect to be happy with either man?

PREJUDICED WITNESS
Dilys Gater

Fleur Rowley finds when she leaves London for her 'author's retreat' in the wilds of North Wales that she is drawn, in spite of herself, into an old tragedy.

GENTLE TYRANT
Lucy Gillen

Working as Ross McAdam's secretary, Laura couldn't imagine why his bitchy ex-wife should see her as a rival.

DEAR CAPRICE
Juliet Gray

Clifford Fortune married Caprice but his brother, Luke, knew the marriage was a mistake. He could allow himself to love Caprice blindly but that would be betraying his own brother.

IN PALE BATTALIONS
Robert Goddard

Leonora Galloway has waited all her life to learn the truth about her father, slain on the Somme before she was born, the truth about the death of her mother and the mystery of an unsolved wartime murder.

A DREAM FOR TOMORROW
Grace Goodwin

In her new position as resident nurse at Coombe Magna, Karen Stevens has to bear the emnity of the beautiful Lisa, secretary to the doctor-on-call.

AFTER EMMA
Sheila Hocken

Following the author's previous auto-biographies — EMMA & I, and EMMA & Co., she relates more of the hilarious (and sometimes despairing) antics of her guide dogs.

A RARE BENEDICTINE
Ellis Peters

Three vintage tales of medieval intrigue and treachery featuring the author's monastic sleuth Brother Cadfael.

POIROT'S EARLY CASES
Agatha Christie

In this collection of eighteen stories, Hercule Poirot begins his celebrated career in crime.

THE SILVER LINK
– THE SILKEN LIE
Lynn Granger

Elspeth is determined to preserve her Scottish heritage and the Elliot name, but running Everanlea, a large hill farm, presents problems.

THE SONG OF THE PINES
Christina Green

Taken to a Greek island as substitute for David Nicholas's secretary, Annie quickly falls prey to the island's charms and to the charms of both Marcus, the Greek, and David himself.

GOODBYE DOCTOR GARLAND
Marjorie Harte

The story of a woman doctor who gave too much to her profession and almost lost her personal happiness.

DIGBY
Pamela Hill

Welcomed at courts throughout Europe, Kenelm Digby was the particular favourite of the Queen of France, who wanted him to be her lover, but the beautiful Venetia was the mainspring of his life.